AT THE MOUTH OF HELL . . .

Bueller and 1st Squad approached the aliens' mound cautiously—unarmed as they were, and walking knowingly to their deaths. The mound—nest? hive?—whatever, loomed like an apartment-building-sized anthill. The surface was ridged and convoluted, a dull blackish gray, with bits of lighter color here and there. As they drew nearer, Bueller saw that the lighter bits were bones, a lot of them skulls, all blended into the surface.

"Damn," somebody said quietly.

There was an oval-shaped entrance with a beaten path leading to it maybe a hundred meters ahead.

"I ain't goin' in there," Ramirez said.

But the trio of air pods buzzing back and forth overhead like dragonflies meant otherwise. As if to confirm this, Bueller's com came to life. "Move in," the voice said.

And to punctuate the command, a thin green plasma beam splashed against the ground behind the squad, digging a small smoking crater into the stony surface. . . .

**Don't miss any of these exciting *Aliens,
Predator,* and *Aliens vs. Predator* adventures
from Bantam Books!**

ALIENS ™

BOOK ONE

EARTH HIVE

Steve Perry

(Based on the Twentieth Century Fox motion pictures, the designs of H. R. Giger, and the graphic novel by Mark Verheiden and Mark A. Nelson.)

A DARK HORSE SCIENCE FICTION NOVEL

BANTAM BOOKS
NEW YORK • TORONTO • LONDON • SYDNEY • AUCKLAND

ALIENS: EARTH HIVE

A Bantam Spectra Book / October 1992

ISBN 0-553-56120-0

Published simultaneously in the United States and Canada

---

*Bantam Books are published by Bantam Books, a division of Random House, Inc.
Its trademark, consisting of the words "Bantam Books" and the portrayal of a
rooster, is Registered in U.S. Patent and Trademark Office and in other countries.
Marca Registrada. Bantam Books, 1540 Broadway, New York, New York 10036.*

PRINTED IN THE UNITED STATES OF AMERICA

OPM   16   15   14   13   12

For Dianne, one more time;
And for Pat Dupre, former harpist
with the Denver Symphony, who saved
my soul in Baton Rouge during the
hippie autumn of 1970

"Fancy thinking the Beast was something you could hunt and kill . . ."

—William Golding,
Lord of the Flies

1

Even inside her bulky E-suit, Billie could feel the cold night bite at her. Sure, the land crawler blocked most of the icy wind, and they had pulled one of the crawler's portable heaters and turned it up full, pretending it was a campfire, but it was still cold. It was the best they could do—there wasn't any wood on the planet Ferro, and if there had been they sure as shit wouldn't be *burning* it. Wood was worth more per gram than platinum on this world. How the guys in the vids could chop it up and waste it was unreal.

The frozen wind howled like some kind of unhappy beast as it blew past the squat form of the crawler; the song changed to a whistle where it flowed over the tractor's sharp treads. The sounds were eerie. Every now and then through a patchy break in the roiling and thick clouds, the stars gleamed briefly, hard pinpricks against a dead-black curtain, glittering like diamonds caught in a laser beam. Even without the clouds it would have been dim; Ferro had no moons.

Well, right, so it wasn't comfortable out here, but at least the three of them weren't stuck inside the colony with the do-nothing dweebs, bored half stupid.

"Okay," Mag said, "what else we s'posed to do here? We ate the RTE rations and sang that fool song about logs and holes in the bottom of the sea. This is terminal droll, Carly."

At twelve, Mag was a year younger than Billie and Carly, and she always had a smart crack about everything.

Billie shivered inside her E-suit. "Yeah, juice brain, what else was on that old disc about camping?"

"If you two dweebs will shut up, I'll tell you."

Mag slapped herself over the heart. "Oh, killer clever," Mag said. "Got me."

"They used to tell stories," Carly said, pretending to ignore her. "Like ghosts and monsters and shit."

"Fine," Mag said. "So, tell us one."

Carly went off on a ramble about vampires and ghosts and Billie knew she'd pulled it from an old entcom file. Even so, it was one thing to see the vid in your cube, all warm and well lit, another thing to hear the story out here a klick away from the Main Building in the dark and cold and all. Spooky.

Windblown hail spattered briefly, like a handful of gravel tossed at them, but stopped just as Carly hit the climax of her story.

"—and every year, one of the survivors of that horrible night goes crazy—and now it's *my* turn!"

Mag and Billie both jumped as Carly lunged at them.

Then all three began to giggle.

"Okay, Mag, you're up."

"Yeah, okay. There was this old witch, see . . . ?"

Halfway through Mag's tale some ice pellets fell and bounced around. One must have gotten into the heater's circuits. The unit flashed brightly, blew its fuse, and died. As the glow faded, the only light they had left was from the stars and the crawler's LEDs. The night moved in on them, and the cold and the dark both thickened. All of a sudden, the Main Building seemed a lot farther than a klick away. More hail showered on them. Billie shivered, and it wasn't just from the cold.

"Aw, shit. Look at that. My dad is gonna be pissed we shorted out the aux heater. I'm getting into the crawler," Mag said.

"Come on, finish your story."

"Forget it. My ears are about to freeze off."

"Well, we have to at least let Billie tell one."

Carly nodded at Billie. "Your turn."

"I think Mag is right, let's get in the crawler."

"Come on, Billie, don't do a guppy-up on us."

Billie took a deep breath and blew out a cloud of cold fog. She remembered her dreams. They wanted something scary? Fine. "Okay. I got one for you.

"There are these . . . things. Nobody knows what planet they come from, but they showed up one day on Rim. They're the color of black glass, they're three meters long and have fangs as big as your fingers. They have acid for blood—you cut one and if it bleeds on you, it burns right through to the bone. Only you can't really cut them, 'cause they have skin as hard as a deep spacer's hull. All they do is eat and reproduce, they're like giant bugs, and they can bite through tool alloy, their teeth are diamond hard. . . ."

"Oh, wow," Carly said.

"If they catch you, you're *lucky* if they kill you," Billie continued. "Because if they *don't* kill you right off, it's worse than death. They put a baby monster inside of you, they ram it down your throat, and it grows in your body, grows until its teeth get sharp enough, and then it chews its way out, through meat and bone, it digs a hole in your guts—"

"Creesto, yuk!" Carly said.

Mag slapped herself over the chest.

Billie paused, waiting for the wisecrack.

But Mag said, "I—I don't . . . feel too good. . . ."

"Come on, Mag," Carly said. "This is moron-ville—"

"N-n-no, I—my stomach—ow!"

Billie swallowed, her throat dry. "Mag?"

"Ahh, it hurts!"

Mag slapped at her chest, as if she were trying to smash a rock beetle with her hand.

Suddenly the E-suit bulged over Mag's solar plexus, like a fist trying to punch through a sheet of rubber. The suit stretched impossibly.

"Aaahhh!" Mag's scream washed over Billie.

"Mag! No!" Billie stood, backed away.

Carly reached for Mag. "What is it?"

Mag's suit stretched again. Tore open. Blood fountained outward, bits of flesh sprayed, and a snakelike thing the size of Billie's arm flashed needle-pointed teeth in the dim starlight as it emerged from the dying girl.

Carly yelled, her voice breaking. She tried to back away, but the monster shot from Mag to Carly like a rocket. It fastened those terrible fangs on to her throat. It bit. Her blood looked black under the starlight as it spewed into the night. Her scream turned into a gurgle.

"No!" Billie screamed. "No! It was a dream! It wasn't real! It *wasn't*! No—!"

Billie struggled up from sleep screaming.

The medic leaned over her. She was on a pressor bed, and the fields held her firmly to the cushion like a giant hand. She struggled, but the harder she tried, the stronger the field became.

"No!"

"Easy, Billie, easy! It's only a dream! You're fine, everything is okay!"

Billie's breath came in gasps. Her heart pounded, she could feel her pulse in her temples as she stared up at Dr. Jerrin. The indirect light gleamed on the sterile white walls and ceiling of the medical center room. Only a dream. Just like the others.

"I'll get you a soporific patch," Jerrin began.

She shook her head, the pressor field would allow that much. "No. No, I'm okay now."

"You sure?"

He had a kindly face; he was old enough to be

Billie's grandfather. He had treated her for years, ever since she'd come to Earth. For the dreams. They weren't all the same, usually she dreamed about Rim, the world on which she'd been born. It had been thirteen years since the nuclear accident that had destroyed the colony on Rim, almost a decade since she left Ferro. And still the nightmares came, carrying her on wild and uncontrollable gallops through her nights. The drugs didn't help. Counseling, hypnosis, biofeedback, brainwave synthesization, nothing helped.

Nothing could stop the dreams.

He let her up and she moved to the sink to wash her face. The mirror frowned back at her. Her reflection was medium height, slim and tight from all the compulsive time she spent in the exercise chair. Her hair, usually cut short, had grown almost to her shoulders, the pale brown of it straight and nearly ash-colored. Pale blue eyes over a straight nose, a mouth just a hair too big. Not an ugly face, but nothing to cross the room to get a better look at. Not ugly, but cursed, sure enough. Some god somewhere must have her in his sights. Billie wished she knew why.

"Buddha, they're all around us!" Quinn yelled.

Wilks felt the sweat rolling down his spine under the spidersilk armor. The light was too dim, the helmet lamp didn't do shit, it was hard to see what was happening around them. The infrared wasn't working worth a crap, either. "Shut the fuck up, Quinn! Maintain your field of fire, we're gonna be fine!"

"Oh, fuck, Corp, they got the sarge!" That from Jasper, one of the other remaining marines. There had been twelve of them in the squad. Now there were four. "What are we gonna do?"

Wilks had the little girl in one arm, his carbine in the other hand. The little girl was crying. "Easy, honey," he said. "We're gonna be fine. We're going back to the ship, everything is gonna be okay."

Ellis, bringing up the rear, swore in Swahili. "Oh, man, oh, man, what the hell *are* these things?" he said.

It was a rhetorical question. Nobody fucking knew.

The heat pounded at Wilks, the air was cloying, it smelled like something dead left too long in the sunshine. Where the things had gotten to the walls of the place the flat everlast plastic had been overlaid with a thick and convoluted blackish-gray substance. It looked like some mad sculptor had covered the walls with loops of intestine. The twisted coils were as hard as plastecrete, but they put out warmth, some kind of organic decay, maybe. It was like an oven in here, but wetter.

Behind him, Quinn's caseless carbine came alive again, the sound of the shots battering Wilks's ears with muted echoes.

"Quinn!"

"There's a shitload of 'em behind us, Corp!"

"Shoot for targets," Wilks ordered. "Triplets only! We don't have enough ammo to waste on full auto suppressive fire!"

Ahead the corridor branched, but the pressure doors had come down and sealed both exits. A flashing light and Klaxon blinked and hooted, and a computer-chip voice kept repeating a warning that the reactor was approaching meltdown.

They were going to have to cut their way out, fast, or get slaughtered by those things. Or else fried into radioactive ash. Great fucking choice.

"Jasper, hold the kid."

"No!" the little girl yelled.

"I gotta open the door," Wilks said. "Jasper will take care of you."

The black marine moved in, grabbed the girl. She clutched at him like a baby monkey does its mother.

Wilks turned to the door. Pulled his plasma cutter from his belt, triggered it. The white-hot jet of plasma flashed out in a line as long as his forearm. He shoved the cutter against the fail-safe lock, waved it back and forth. The lock was made of tripolystacked carbon, but it wasn't designed to withstand the heat of a star. The carbon annealed, bubbled, and ran like water under the plasma jet.

The door slid up.

One of the monsters stood there. It lunged at Wilks, a long, toothed rod shooting from its open mouth like a spear at his face. Saliva dripped from its jaws in jellylike strings.

"Fuck!" Wilks dodged to his right and swung the plasma cutter up reflexively. The line caught the thing's neck, a neck that looked much too thin to support the impossibly large head. How could something like this even stand up? It didn't make any sense—

The alien creatures were tough, but the plasma was hot enough to melt industrial diamond. The head fell off, bounced on the floor. It kept on trying to bite Wilks, jaws oozing slime as it snapped at him. Didn't even know it was dead.

"Move it, people! And watch it, the damned thing is still dangerous!"

Jasper screamed.

"Jasper!"

One of the things had him, and it crunched his head like a cat biting a mouse. The little girl—!

"Wilks! Help! Help!"

Another one of the monsters had the girl, it was moving away with her. Wilks twisted, pointed his weapon at it. Realized that if he shot it, the blood would be an acid shower that would kill the child. He'd seen that blood eat through armor that would stop a 10mm caseless cold. He dropped his aim lower, pointed the carbine at its legs. It couldn't run if it didn't have any feet—

The corridor was full of the things, Quinn opened up, his carbine on full auto, blasting. Armor-piercing and explosive rounds tore through the monsters, spanged from the walls, the stink of propellant filled the air—

Ellis opened up with his flamer, and a stream of fire painted the corridor, splashing from the aliens and running in molten gobs down the intestined wall—

"Help!" the little girl cried. "Oh, please, help!"

Oh, God!

"No!"

Wilks came awake, sweat drenching his hair and

face, running into his eyes. His issue coverall was wet. Oh, man.

He sat up. He was still in the cell, on the thin bunk, the dark plastic walls securely in place.

The door slid open. A guard robot was there, two and a half meters tall on its tractor treads, gleaming under the jail corridor's lights. The robot's electronic voice said, "Corporal Wilks! Front and center!"

Wilks rubbed at his eyes. Even a military brig with all its security couldn't keep the dreams out.

Nothing could stop the dreams.

"Wilks!"

"Yeah, what?"

"You are to report to MILCOM HQ, OTD."

"Fuck you, tinhead. I got two more days to serve on the S&D."

"You wish, pal," the bot said. "Your high-rank friends say otherwise. Up-levels wants you, OTD."

"What high-rank friends?" Wilks asked.

One of the other prisoners in the multi-unit cell, a fat man from Benares, said, "What friends, period?"

Wilks stared at the line bot. Now, why would the glitter want to see him on the double? Anytime rank started rumbling, it usually meant trouble for the grunts. He felt his gut churn, and it wasn't just the dregs of the chem-binge he'd gone on, either. Whatever this was, it wasn't good.

"Let's go, marine," the bot said. "I am to escort you to MILCOM HQ soonest."

"Lemme shower and clean up first."

"Negative, mister. They said, 'Soonest.' "

The burn scar that mostly covered the left half of his face began to itch suddenly. Oh, shit. Not just bad, but *real* bad.

Now what did they think he'd done?

2

There was a lot of trash orbiting Earth.

In the hundred years since the first satellites had lifted, careless astronauts or construction crews had lost bolts, tools, and other chunks of hardware. The small stuff, some of it whipping around at fifteen klicks a second relative, could punch a nasty hole in anything less dense than full-sheath armor, and that included people inside a ship coming or going. Even a chip of paint could dig a crater when it hit. While this was a danger to ships, most of the little stuff burned up on reentry; what didn't was collected by special robot rigs everybody called dust mops.

For a time there was a real risk that the big stuff would get to the ground—part of a construction ship flamed down and killed a hundred thousand people on the Big Island once, and also made Kona coffee exceedingly rare. Because of that and similar incidents, somebody finally realized there was a problem with all the orbiting junk. Laws were passed, and now anything bigger than a man got tagged and swept. And rather than create a new agency, the work was passed on to an organization that already existed.

This was why the Coast Guard cutter *Dutton* hung in high orbit over North Africa, starlight glistening on its armored boron-carbon hull, its crew of two yawning as they moved in to tag a derelict ship. Garbage Control's flight computer said this heap was about to start its fall, and before that happened, the thing had to be probed, checked for anybody who might be camping on it, then blasted into pieces small enough for the dust mops to collect. SOP.

"Probe ready to launch," Ensign Lyle said.

Next to him, the cutter's captain, Commander Barton, nodded. "Stand by and . . . launch probe."

Lyle touched the control. "Probe away. Telemetry is green. Visuals on, sensors on, one-second burn."

The tiny robot ship rocketed toward the battered freight hauler, feeding electronic information to the cutter behind it.

"Maybe this one is full of platinum ingots," Lyle said.

"Yeah, right. And maybe it's raining on the moon."

"What's the matter, Bar? You don't want to be rich?"

"Sure. And I want to spend ten years in the CG

pen fighting off the yard monsters, too. Unless you figured out a way to shut down the blue box?"

Lyle laughed. The blue box recorded everything that went on in the cutter, plus all the probe input. Even if the ship *was* full of platinum, there was no way to hide it from Command. And military officers didn't get salvage rights. "Well, not exactly," Lyle said. "But if we had a few million credits, we could *hire* somebody who might."

"Yeah, your mother," Barton said.

Lyle glanced at the computer flat screen. It was cheap hardware; the Navy had full holographics but the Guard still had to make do with the bottom-of-the-line Sumatran Guild electronics. The probe's retros flamed as it reached the hulk. "Here we are. Is that good flying, or what?"

Barton grunted. "Look at the hatch. It's bulged outward."

"Explosion, you think?" Lyle said.

"Dunno. Let's open this can up."

Lyle tapped at his keyboard. The probe extruded a universal hatch key and inserted it into the lock.

"No luck. Lock's shot," Lyle said.

"I'm not blind, I can see that. Pop it."

"Hope the inner hatch is closed."

"Come on, this piece of crap has been up here for at least sixty years. Anybody on it would be dead of old age. There ain't no air in there and if by some miracle somebody *is* home, they're in a suspension tank. And aside from *that*, this thing has about thirty minutes before it hits enough atmosphere to boil lead. Pop it."

Lyle shrugged. Touched controls.

The probe attached a small charge to the hatch and retroed back a hundred meters. The charge flared silently in the vacuum and the hatch shattered.

"Knock, knock. Anybody home?"

"Go see. And try not to bang the probe up too bad this time."

"That wasn't my fault," Lyle said. "One of the retros was plugged."

"So you say."

The tiny robot ship moved in through the opening in the derelict ship.

"Inner hatch is open."

"Good. Saves time. Move it in."

The probe's halogens lit as it moved into the ship.

The radiation alarm chimed on the computer's screen. "Kinda hot in there," Lyle said.

"Yep, hope you like your soypro well done."

"Mmm. I guess anybody in this baby would be toast by now. We'll have to give the probe a bath when it gets back."

"Chreesto, look at that!" Barton said.

What had been a man floated just ahead of the probe. The hard radiation had killed the bacteria that would have rotted him, and the cold had preserved what the vacuum hadn't sucked out of him. He looked like a leather prune. He was naked.

"Lordy, lordy," Lyle said. "Hey, check the wall behind him." He touched a control and the visuals enhanced and enlarged. Something was written on the bulkhead in smeary brown letters: KILL US ALL, it said.

"Damn, is that written in blood? Looks like blood to me."

"You want an analysis?"

"Never mind. We got us a flip ship."

Lyle nodded. They'd heard about them, though he himself had never opened one. Somebody went nuts and wasted everybody else. Opened a port and let the air out, or maybe flooded the ship with radiation, like this one. A quick death or a slow one, but death, sure enough. Lyle shivered.

"Find a terminal and see if you can download the ship's memory. The meter is running here."

"If the batteries are still good. Oops. Got motion on the detector."

"I see it. I don't believe it, but I see it. Nobody can possibly be alive, even somebody in a full rad suit would cook in this tub—"

"There it is. It's just a cargo carrier."

A short, squat robot crawled along a line of Velcro against the ceiling.

"We must have jolted it awake when we blew the hatch."

"Yeah, right. Get the memory."

The probe floated toward a control panel.

"Damn, look at those holes in the deck. Looks like something dissolved the plastic. Radiation wouldn't do that, would it?"

"Who knows? Who cares? Just dump the memory and pull the probe so we can blow this sucker. I have a date tonight and I don't want any overtime."

"You're the commander."

The probe connected to the control board. The

ship's power was almost gone, but sufficient to download the memory.

"Coming in," Lyle said. "Here's the ID scan, onscreen."

"No surprises here," Barton said. "Type five nuke drive, lotta deep-space time, bad shields, dead core. No wonder they junked this bucket. That's it. Shove it sunward, set the 10-CA and let's go home."

Lyle touched more controls. The probe placed the small clean atomic against a wall where it adhered. "Okay, three minutes to—aw, shit!"

The screen went blank.

"What did you do?"

"I didn't do *any*thing! The camera's gone out."

"Switch to memory drive. We lose another probe and the Old Man'll chew our asses to pulp."

Lyle touched a button. The computer took over the probe. Since it had memorized every centimeter of the flight in, it could retrace the flight and bring the probe back.

"It's clear," Lyle said a moment later. "Burning more fuel than it should, though."

"Maybe it snagged on something coming out. Doesn't matter."

"Probe docking. Outer hatch open. Let me see if I can get an eye on the sucker and see why it's wallowing so bad." Lyle ran his practiced hands over the controls.

"Holy fuck!" Barton said.

Lyle just stared. What the hell was that? Some kind of *thing* sat on the probe as it approached the ship. It looked like a reptile, no, a giant bug. Wait, it had to be some kind of suit, no way it could live in vac without a suit—

"Close the hatch!" Barton yelled.

"Too late! It's inside."

"Flood the bay with antirad! Pump the air out! Blow it back through the fucking door!"

A clang vibrated through the ship. Like a hammer smashing metal.

"It's trying to open the inner hatch!"

Frantically Lyle tapped controls. "Antirad spray on full! Evacuation pumps on!"

The banging continued.

"Okay, okay, don't worry, it can't get in. The hatch is locked. Nobody can break through a sealed boron-carbon hatch with his bare hands!"

Something crashed, ringing loudly. Then came the sound spacers fear more than anything: air rushing out.

"Close the outer hatch, goddammit!"

But the dropping air pressure tugged at Lyle. The cabin was filled with loose items being sucked toward the rear of the cutter. Light pens, coffee cups, a hard-copy magazine fluttering madly. He lunged at the controls, missed the emergency button, lunged again.

Barton, also half out of his chair, stabbed at the red button, but hit the computer override instead. The ship went to manual drive.

The cabin pressure raced toward zero. A hatch-sized hole blew air into space real damned fast. Lyle's eyes bulged, began to bleed. One eardrum popped. He screamed, but found the control for the external hatch.

"I got it! I got it!"

The outer hatch cycled shut. Emergency air tanks kicked on. The faux gravity pulled the two men back toward their seats. "Goddammit! Goddammit!" Barton said.

"It's okay, it's okay, it's closed!"

"Coast Guard Control, this is the cutter *Dutton!*" Barton began. "We have a situation here!"

"Oh, *man!*" Lyle said.

Barton twisted.

The thing stood right fucking there!

It had *teeth!* It came toward them. It looked hungry.

Barton tried to get up, fell, and hit the drive control. The ship was still on manual. The drive kicked on. The acceleration threw the monster backward, drove Lyle and Barton into their seats. Even though they couldn't move, the thing somehow managed to drag itself onward.

It was a nightmare. It couldn't be real.

The thing ripped chunks out of Lyle's seat as it pulled him from the chair. Blood sprayed as its clawed hands punctured his shoulders. It opened its mouth and a rod shot out, so fast Barton could hardly see it. The rod buried itself in Lyle's head like his skull was putty. Blood and brain tissue splashed. Lyle screamed in total terror.

The cutter, still under acceleration, headed directly toward the radioactive hulk in front of it.

The monster jerked that hellish thing from Lyle's skull. It made a sucking sound, like a foot pulled out of mud. The creature turned toward Barton.

Barton drew breath to scream, but the sound never came out—

At that instant the cutter smashed into the scuttled freighter—

—and the bomb the probe had set went off.

Both ships were destroyed in the explosion. Virtually everything was shattered into tiny bits that spiraled in a long loop toward Sol.

Everything except the blue box.

Wilks stared at the screen as it washed white.

Amazing how well the blue boxes were armored, to survive even a close atomic blast like that.

He looked at the guard bot. "Okay, I've seen it."

"Let's go," the bot said.

They were alone in a conference room in MIL-COM HQ. Wilks stood, and the bot led the way. If he'd had a gun, he would have shot the bot and tried to run. Yeah. Right.

As they walked along the corridor, Wilks put it together. So this was why they'd never kicked him out of the Corps. It was only a matter of time before humans stumbled across the aliens again. They hadn't wanted to believe him about what had happened on Rim, but the truth machines wouldn't let them off the hook that easy. The brain strainers had pulled it out of him, and the Corps never threw anything away that might be useful someday.

His belly clenched around a cold knot, like somebody had jammed a blade of liquid nitrogen into his guts. The bomb on Rim hadn't gotten them all. The military found itself in need of an expert on these things and Corporal Wilks was what it had. Probably didn't make them very happy, but they would make do.

He wasn't looking forward to this meeting. It certainly wasn't going to do him any good. Not at all.

3

Salvaje's place was almost directly under the huge reactor shield for the Southern Hemisphere Power Grid Switching Station. The PGSS field was big enough so it sometimes created its own weather. Mostly that was rain. Day and night, steady, unrelieved, dreary-as-shit rain. The building was eon-plas prefab, proof against the more or less constant downpour, a dull gray material that blended in against a sky the color of melted lead. It was a good place to hide. Nobody came here unless they had a reason, even the ground police avoided the rain when they could.

Pindar the holotech splashed through puddles, ankle deep despite the drainage pumps' attempts to clear the water. If Salvaje didn't have so much spare money he was willing to part with, Pindar would have avoided this scum hole. The building walls were thick with mold, even the retardant paint couldn't stop it, and there were rumors that you could catch a mutant strain of flu here that would kill you before you could get to a medic—which wouldn't help anyhow because even recombinant antivirals couldn't touch the stuff. Nice.

The door slid open on creaky runners as Pindar walked up the incline to Salvaje's place.

"You're late," came the ghostly voice from within.

Pindar stepped inside, stripped off the osmotic rainfilm that kept him dry, dropped the torn bits of spiderweb-thin plastic onto the floor. "Yeah, well, between my day job and this shit, it's lucky I can find time to sleep."

"I care nothing for your sleep. I pay well."

Pindar looked at Salvaje. He was ordinary enough. Medium height, hair slicked straight back in some kind of electrostatic hold, a little beard and mustache. He could have been thirty or fifty; he had one of those faces that don't seem to age much. He wore a plain black coverall and flexboots. Pindar wasn't sure what a holy man ought to look like, but Salvaje sure wasn't it.

"There," Salvaje said, pointing.

Pindar saw the cam on a table. "Damn, where'd you get that antique? It looks like an old ship's monitor—"

"Where I got it is not important. Can you use it to tie us into the Nets?"

"Señor, I can tie you into the Nets with a toaster and a couple of microwave cooker circuit boards. I am a very good technician."

Salvaje said nothing, only stared at Pindar with

those cold gray eyes of his. Pindar repressed a
shudder. Gave him the crawlies when he did that.
"Sí, I can put you on the air. But visual and auditory
only. No sublims, no subsonics, no olfactories. Be
pretty tame compared to what your competition is
throwing at the GU."

"The Great Unwashed will hear the truth of my
message without trickery. And they will see the
image of the True Messiah. Such things will be
enough. Behold!"

Salvaje touched a control on an old projector on
the table next to him and a hologram shimmered to
life behind him.

"Madre de Dios!" Pindar said softly.

The image was perhaps three meters from the tip
of its pointed, spiky tail to the top of its banana-
shaped and grotesque head. If it had eyes, they
seemed recessed just behind twin rows of needle-
tipped teeth. Pindar stepped to one side and saw
what appeared to be thick external ribs jutting from
the thing's back, and overall, it looked as if some
god playing a joke had created a manlike thing born
of giant insects. The monster was a dull black or
dark gray, and Pindar would not wish to meet such
a thing under any circumstances. He didn't know
what the Messiah was supposed to look like, either,
but he would bet all the iron in the Asteroid Belt
that this wasn't it.

"I can put you on the air in five minutes," Pindar
said, bending to pick up the antique camera. "Along
with your . . . messiah. It is your money. But I
wonder that anyone will look upon this thing and

think it might deliver them, señor. I myself would expect to see it in Hades."

"Do not blaspheme about that which you do not understand, technician."

Pindar shrugged. He accessed the camera's computer, tied it into a shunt, and rigged a relay transmitter. He moved quickly to the power unit and control console, tapping stolen codes into an orbiting broadcast satellite. He held off on the last digit, then turned to Salvaje. "When I input the final number, you will have three minutes before the WCC locks its trace of our signal. Two more minutes and they will find the dish I hid in Madras, and two minutes after that they will find this place. Best you hold your transmission to five minutes. I have an automatic cut off thirty seconds after that. I will have to find another bounce dish if you wish to broadcast again."

"*Esta no importa,*" Salvaje said.

Pindar shrugged. "Your money."

Salvaje reached up, as if to stroke the dreadful image of the hologram floating in the air behind him. His fingers passed through the image. "Others will have heard the call. I must speak to them."

Crazy as a shithouse rat, Pindar thought. But of this he did not speak aloud. "All right. In four seconds. Three. Two. One." He input the final number.

Salvaje smiled into the camera's lens. "Good day, fellow seekers. I have come to you with the Great Truth. The coming of the True Messiah . . ."

Pindar shook his head. He would sooner worship his dog than this hideous image, which had to be a

computer simulation. Nothing could really look like
that.

The patient cafeteria was nearly empty, a dozen
or so of the inmates shuffling their drug-calmed
ways through the line with soft plastic trays. Billie
moved in her own chemical fog, feeling tired, but
unable to rest.

Sasha sat at a table next to the holoprojection
chair, using a fork made of linear plastic to stir
some ugly noodles around on her plate. The tableware was strong enough to lift the food but would
curl up like cardboard if you tried to stick somebody
with it. Somebody like yourself.

"Hey, Billie," Sasha said. "Check out Deedee,
she's switching channels on the 'jector every three
seconds. Why, I think that girl is mentally dis-
turbed!"

Sasha laughed. Billie knew Sasha's history. She
had pushed her father into a vat of jewelry cleaning
acid when she was nine. She'd been here for eleven
years because every time they asked her whether
she'd do it again if she had the chance, she grinned
and told them sure. Every day of the week and twice
on Sunday.

Billie glanced at Deedee. The girl was gazing at
the 'jector as if hypnotized. The tiny holograms
blinked as she changed the channels. With four or
five hundred choices, it would take even Deedee a
while to see them all.

"C'mon, have a seat. Try some of this worm puke,
it's real good."

Billie sat, almost collapsing.

"You on blues again?"

Billie sighed. "Greens."

"Crap, what'd you do, strangle a nurse?"

"The dreams."

Billie glanced at the tiny viewer in front of Deedee. A deep-space ship flew across the void. Blink. A car chase on a multilane surface road. Blink. A documentary on feral elves. Blink.

"C'mon, Billie," Sasha said, "you only have what, a month left until your hearing?"

"I won't skate this time either, Sash. They can't figure it out. They say my folks died in an explosion. I know better. I was *there*!"

"Ease up, kid. The monitors—"

"Hey, *fuck* the monitors!" Billie shoved her plate across the table, scattering the safety tableware and the noodles. The rubbery plate fell to the cushioned floor, bounced, but made hardly any sound. "They can send a ship a hundred light-years away to another system, they can make an android from amino soup and plastic, but they can't cure me of nightmares!"

Attendants appeared as if by magic, but Billie's rage couldn't stand any longer against the sedatives in her system. She slumped.

Behind her, Deedee said quietly, "Hold channel."

The image of a man with slicked-back hair and a smallish beard shined in the air before her. And behind him, behind him was—was—

"—join us, my friends," the man's voice spoke into the speaker implanted behind Deedee's mastoid bone. "Join the Church of Immaculate Incubation. Receive the ultimate communion. Become one with the True Messiah. . . ."

Deedee smiled as the attendants came and helped Billie to her feet. Billie didn't see the True Messiah as she left.

"Dammit, let go!"

Then somebody pressed a green patch to her carotid and Billie stopped even that much of struggle.

Wilks and the robot reached the security door leading into MILCOM HQ Intel One. A scanning laser tapped a red dot against his eye and by the time he had finished blinking, the door's comp had IDed him and begun to roll open. The bot said, "Go on in. I'll wait here."

Wilks did as he was told. He felt the pressure of stares against him, knowing he was being watched by computers and probably live guards, that his every move was recorded. Fuck it.

There was only one other door in the corridor, so he couldn't miss it. It opened as he approached. He stepped into the office. Nothing but an oval table, big enough to seat a dozen people, three chairs. Two of the chairs were occupied. In one was a full bird colonel, wearing interior regulations. No combat medals, a desk pilot. He'd be the MI officer in charge. There was an oxymoron, "military intelligence."

The other man was in civilian garb, and he had the look. Wilks would bet a month's pay this guy was a t-bag—Terran Intelligency Agency. Any odds anybody wanted.

"At ease, marine," the colonel said. Wilks wasn't aware that he'd been at attention. Old habits die hard.

Wilks noticed that the colonel, his name tag said "Stephens," kept his hands behind his back. Like maybe he was afraid to touch him.

Not so the civilian. He extended one hand. "Corporal Wilks."

Wilks kept his own hand down. Shake with one of these guys and you might need finger grafts.

The civilian nodded, withdrawing his offer of a handshake.

"You saw the recording," Stephens said.

"I saw it."

"What did you think?"

"I thought the guardsmen were lucky they got blown to atoms when they did."

The colonel and the civilian exchanged quick glances. "This is, ah, Mr. . . . Orona," Stephens said.

Yeah, right, and I'm King George the Second, Wilks thought.

"You ran into these things before, didn't you?" the one they called Orona said.

"Yeah."

"Tell me about it."

"What can I tell you that you don't already know? You've seen the recordings of my 'examination,' haven't you?"

"I want to hear it from you."

"Maybe I don't want to tell it to you."

Stephens glared at him. "Give the man the story, marine. That's an order."

Wilks almost laughed. Or what? You'll toss me in the brig? That's exactly where I'd rather be than here. But if they wanted him to talk, they could pry it out of him, the military had dope that could make a crowbar sing opera. He shrugged.

"All right. I was part of a unit sent to check on a colony on Rim. We'd lost contact with them. We found one survivor, a little girl named Billie. Everybody else had been slaughtered by some kind of alien. Same thing that got the guardsmen.

"One of them got onto the lander when it dusted off. Killed the pilot, crashed it. There were twelve of us in the squad, stuck on the ground. I was the only one who got out, me and the little girl. They shipped her off to live with relatives on Ferro, after they wiped her memory. She was a good kid, considering all the shit she saw. We spent some time awake on the ship before we climbed into the deep freezers. I liked her. She was tough.

"Later I heard there was another nest of the things somewhere, killed another colony. Supposedly a marine and a couple civilians got away from that one, too.

"When I got back, the medics patched me up, then took my brain apart. Only thing was, all of a sudden nobody wanted to know from aliens eating colonists and laying eggs in them. It got buried. Top secret, total wipe like the kid if I opened my mouth. That was more than a dozen years ago.

"That's it. End of story."

"You got a bad attitude, Wilks," Stephens said.

Orona smiled. "Colonel, do you suppose I might have a word with the corporal alone?"

After a moment Stephens nodded. "All right. I'll talk to you later."

He left the room.

Orona smiled. "Now we can talk freely."

Wilks laughed. "What? Do I have 'stupid' tattooed on my forehead? If there isn't a battery of recording gear going full blast right now I'll eat that fucking table. Probably the colonel is in the next room watching in full holographic surround. Give me a break, Orona, or whatever your name really is."

"All right," Orona said. "We'll play it your way. Stop me if I get any of it wrong.

"After you managed to escape from Rim, you spend six months in quarantine, to make sure you weren't infected with some kind of alien virus or bacteria. Nobody even tried to see you, no personal visits, nada. You wouldn't let them reconstruct your face."

"Women love scars," Wilks said. "Makes 'em sympathetic."

Orona continued. "When you were put back on active duty, you turned into a chemhound. Nine arrests and subsequent terms in the brig for Stoned and Disorderly. Three for assault, two for damage to property, one for attempted homicide."

"Guy had a big mouth," Wilks offered.

"I specialize in genetics, Corporal, but anybody who's ever taken a psych course can see you're on a one-way trip down the reaction tubes."

"So? It's my life. What do you care?"

"Before those two Coast Guard clowns blew themselves up, they downloaded the derelict's data banks. We have a trajectory of that old ship. We know where it came from before it came home to die."

"Ask me if I care."

"Oh, you should, Corporal. You're going there. Whatever your problems are don't matter. I need a specimen of the thing the Coast Guard found. You're going to bring me one."

"I won't volunteer for it."

"Oh, but you will." Orona grinned.

Wilks blinked. Something unhappy roiled around in Wilks's belly, like a trapped beast wanting to get out. While he was still wondering if he were about to vomit whatever was left from his most recent meal, Orona hit him with another one.

"You know that little girl you rescued? She's here. On Earth. In a mental center. They keep her sedated and run a lot of tests on her. She has these nightmares, you see. Apparently the brainwipe didn't completely take. She remembers things, in her dreams.

"You could wind up in a place like that, if you don't do the right thing."

Billie was here? He hadn't thought he'd ever see her again. He had been curious about her more than once. She was the only person who'd seen those things the way he had, least the only one he knew about. He stared at Orona. Then he nodded. If they wanted you, they would get you, he'd been in the Corps long enough to know that. He would go or damn sure wish he had. There were worse things than dying.

He took a deep breath. "Okay," he said. "I'll go."

Orona smiled, and when he did, it reminded Wilks of the aliens.

Damn.

4

Billie slept. She could hear voices in her dream, a distant overlay of ghostly sound wound among the shimmering and frightful images.

"—dreaming again. What'd you give her?"

A door loomed in front of Billie, partially open. Behind the door, blackness. Eyes gleamed in the dark there, and light flashed briefly on rows of serrated teeth.

"—thirty of Trinomine—"

The undulating door swung wide, creaking loudly. A kind of . . . presence oozed through. Billie couldn't see it clearly. . . .

"—thirty? That's twice the usual dosage. Aren't you worried about brain damage?"

The presence coalesced, forming a quavery image. Black, tall, toothed. The monster. It grinned at Billie. Gnashed those teeth. Moved toward her.

Billie was frozen. Couldn't even turn away as it came for her. She opened her mouth to scream—

"—well, that's a risk, isn't it? She's already halfway insane and none of the conventional therapies work. Besides, medical-grade androids have taken up to forty milligrams without significant damage—"

The monster reached for her. Opened its mouth. Slowly a toothed rod extruded itself from that hellish mouth. Came toward her, slow, oh, so slow, but she . . . couldn't . . . move. . . .

"—she's not an android, though—"

"—might as well be—"

A hand touched Billie's shoulder.

Billie awoke, her heart thudding rapidly. She was sweating hard.

It was Sasha.

"Oh, Sash. What are you doing here?"

"You have a visitor, Doc sent me to tell you."

"A visitor? I don't know anybody on Earth except the medics and the inmates here."

Sasha shrugged. "Doc says somebody is in V4 for you. You want me to go along?"

"No. I can handle it."

The truth was, she didn't feel particularly adept at the moment; the drugs coursed through her system and the latest nightmare still vibrated in her memory. But if she was ever going to get out of this place, she had to look as if she were in control.

Billie found her way down the hall, was admitted

into the visitor area. The door to V4 scanned her
and admitted her into the "private" room. Inside
was a monitor inset into the right wall and a single
form-chair facing a fully polarized wall that shined
like a black mirror.

Billie sat.

Who could it be?

The monitor came to life. Onscreen was a com-
puterized image of a kindly, white-haired grand-
mother. Her chip-voice when she spoke was also
kindly, but full of quiet authority. Billie also knew
the voice was full of subsonics and sublims designed to calm and soothe a listener, as well as
engender obedience.

"You are being monitored," Grandma said. "And
any discussion of hospital therapy will result in
termination of this visitation." Grandma smiled,
forming lines at the corners of her eyes. "Visitation
is a privilege and not a right. You are allowed ten
minutes. Is this understood?"

"Yeah, right."

"Very good. Enjoy your visit."

Grandma smiled again and faded from the
screen. A small red dot pulsed in her place, remind-
ing Billie that the conversation was being recorded
and observed.

The polarized wall faded from black to clear.

A man, one side of his face scarred, sat in the
chair two meters away from her. He wore a military
uniform.

Who . . . ?

"Hello, Billie."

It was as if somebody suddenly slammed a fist

into the side of her head. The jolt rocked her physically. Billie jerked and stared as a memory they'd tried to take away from her swam to the surface like a whale needing air.

It was him! The man who'd always saved her in her dreams.

"Wilks!"

"Yeah. How they treating you in here?"

"You—you're *real*!"

"Last time I looked, yeah."

"Oh, God, Wilks!"

"I wasn't sure you'd remember me."

"You—you look . . . different."

He touched the scars on his face. "Colonial Marine surgeons. Buncha butchers."

"Wh-what are you doing here?"

"They told me you were in this place. I figured I had to see you, once I found out you were having the dreams, too."

"About the monsters."

"Yeah. I don't sleep that well myself. Haven't since Rim."

"It was real, wasn't it?"

"Oh, yeah. It was real. They had me, I'm in as long as they keep reactivating my secrecy clause, but you were a civilian. They decided to wipe you, but it didn't work, least not all the way."

Billie slumped, but at the same time felt a sense of relief like none she'd ever known. It was *real*! She wasn't crazy! The dreams were memories, trying to get out!

* * *

Wilks stared at the kid. Well, she wasn't really a kid anymore, was she? Turned out to be a nice-looking woman, even in the hospital whites and obviously stoned on whatever they gave her.

He wasn't sure why he'd come, except that maybe she was the only other person who would understand the dreams he kept having. He'd tried to track her down a long time ago, along with the other marine and the civilians who'd escaped from the second bug nest, but they'd all been carefully hidden away. Probably in some medical center like this one, or on some outpost a dozen light-years from anywhere. Or maybe they were dead.

"Why did you come?" she asked.

He pulled his thoughts back to the young woman on the other side of the thick, clear plastic wall. "They found what they think is the homeworld for those . . . things," he said. "They're sending me there with some troops."

A few seconds went past. "To destroy it?"

Wilks smiled, but it was a sour expression. "To collect a 'specimen.' I think MI wants to use the things as some kind of weapon."

"No! You can't let them!"

"Kid, I can't stop them. I'm a corporal." And a drunk and chemhead brawler, he added mentally.

"Get me out of here," she said.

"Huh?"

"I'm not crazy. The memories are real. You can tell them. They're trying to convince me everything I remember is an illusion but you know the truth. Tell them. You saved me before, Wilks, do it again!

They're killing me in here with the drugs, the therapy! I have to get out!"

The monitor screen next to her flowered, and a white-haired old lady appeared there, smiling. "Discussion of therapy is not allowed," she said. "This visit is terminated. Please leave the visiting area immediately."

"Wilks, *please*!"

Wilks found himself standing, his fists clenched.

"Please leave the visiting area immediately," the old lady said.

Billie stood and leapt at the clear wall. She slammed her fists into the hard plastic. "Let me go!"

The door behind her opened and two large men entered. They grabbed Billie. The young woman struggled, but it was no use. The wall began to polarize and darken.

"Hey, fuckheads, let her go!" Wilks yelled. He lunged at the wall, slammed into it. He backed off, threw his shoulder into the wall again. The wall was unmoved.

The monitor on his side of the darkening plastic came to life. The same old woman. "This visit has been terminated. Please exit now. Thank you for coming. Have a nice day."

"Wilks! Help me!" Billie screamed.

Then the sound faded and the wall went totally dark, and she was gone.

Wilks leaned away from the wall. He stared at his hands. "Sorry, kid," he whispered. "I'm sorry."

5

Excerpts from the script of the top-secret audiovisual presentation "Theory of Alien Propagation," by Waidslaw Orona, Ph.D.

Note: This script/compgen AV recording is/are classified military document(s) and require a clearance of __A-1/a__ for reading/viewing. Penalties for illegal uses of this/these document(s) may include Full Brain Reconstruction and/or a fine of up to Cr. 100,000, and/or imprisonment in a Federated Penal Colony for up to twenty-five years.

FADE IN:

COMPUTER GEN PIX: Deep space, a b.g. of stars. Centered is AN ALIEN, sideview, curled into a fetallike ball. MUSIC PLAYS: Wagner's "Ride of the Valkyries."

V.O.

Humans suffer from self-centered notions as to the nature of life.

The Alien slowly uncurls. MUSICAL STING.

V.O. (CONT.)

Humans assume that alien life forms should conform to standards that match our own, including logic and morality.

The Alien is uncurled in its full glory now. Slowly it rotates to face the camera. MUSIC CONTINUES OVER.

V.O. (CONT.)

Even among humans, morality is ignored when expedient. Why should we expect more from an alien life form than we demand from ourselves?

The Alien stretches out its arms and legs and tail so that it becomes a parody of the man's-reach-should-equal-his-height illustration by Da Vinci. PUSH IN SLOWLY. The Alien expands to fill the screen.

V.O. (CONT.)

If we know nothing else, we must know this about aliens: First, they will not be like us. Second, truly understanding them will be almost impossible.

THE ALIEN

fills the screen; DIAL DOWN MUSIC and PUSH THROUGH TO BLACK.

CUT TO:

EXT. ALIEN WORLD—DAY—ESTABLISHING

Here is a bleak, rocky planet. Very little greenery, vast stretches of nothing.

> V.O.
> Judging from the dense exoskeleton of the alien and its demonstrated adaptability, we must assume that its home planet is a harsh, desolate place.

CUT TO:

EXT. HIVE

This is a ridged, antlike mound rearing up from the cleared area around it, a thing composed of alien spittle, laced with local plants and the exoskeletons of alien prey.

> V.O.
> We know from our previous encounters that the aliens have a queen-based hierarchy and that they form hives to protect their eggs and young hatchlings.

INT. HIVE—EGG CHAMBER

The giant QUEEN, monstrous egg sac attached to her rear, deposits eggs on the floor of the chamber.

V.O.

At the proper time, drone workers provide host bodies for the newborns.

TIME CUT TO:

INT. EGG ROOM

A GROUP OF PREY BEASTS held in place by WORKER ALIENS are attacked by HATCHLINGS IN THEIR LARVAL FORM. (These are hand-shaped lumps with fingers and tails, the latter of which wrap around the prey beasts' necks to secure them as the ovipositors are extruded and inserted down the prey's throats. See comp-image #3 for stock footage.)

V.O.

The parasitical breeding process is offensive to some in the scientific community, but completely natural for aliens living in a harsh environment.

CUT TO:

PREY BEAST

Its belly bulges from within. It screams, but silently, (MOS).

V.O.

Birth of the next stage is violent and fatal for the host.

C.U.—PREY'S BELLY

The skin bursts, tissue spews, and A BABY ALIEN, looking like a fat snake with sharp teeth, emerges.

> V.O. (CONT.)
> The young alien chews its way forth, where there may be a battle for dominance with other newly born aliens. We can only speculate at this point.

A GROUP OF BABY ALIENS

rip and tear at each other.

CUT TO:

EXT. HIVE—DAY

Overhead a spaceship ROARS by; below on the ground, A GROUP OF WORKER ALIENS watch the ship.

> V.O.
> How the aliens escape their world is, of course, complete speculation.

THE SHIP

lands and a SUITED FIGURE emerges, carrying assorted collecting gear and a wicked-looking hand weapon.

V.O. (CONT.)
However, it seems likely that some . . . outside force, perhaps a spacefaring species, interacted with the aliens.

THE SUITED FIGURE

returns to the ship, an alien egg inside a clear specimen bottle. From the size of the egg compared to the Collector, it is apparent that the Collector is much larger than a man, perhaps three times so.

CUT TO:

INT. COLLECTOR'S SPACESHIP

The Collector approaches the alien egg. Leans over it. The egg's portal flaps splay open. The Collector peers into the egg's interior.

V.O.
A small mistake in dealing with such predatory creatures would, of course, prove to be dangerous in the extreme. Probably fatal.

CUT TO:

EXT. COLLECTOR'S SPACESHIP

The ship lies crashed upon some world, fog swirling about it. PUSH IN AND THROUGH TO:

INT. COLLECTOR'S SHIP

The skeleton of the Collector, its chest burst open from within, sits in the control seat of the ship. In the b.g. are THREE HUMANS IN SPACESUITS. Light beams play over the dead giant as the humans examine it.

> V.O.
> Humans rely on technology to the point where they believe it has made them invincible. When dealing with creatures who have adapted to extremely hostile environments, such a belief can also prove dangerous.

EXT. CORPORATION LANDER

The lander lifts from the planet's surface.

CLOSER—ON THE LANDER

Clutching a strut on the lander's underside is AN ALIEN.

> V.O. (CONT.)
> Because an unsuited human cannot survive in the vacuum of space does not mean that some other complex life form cannot.

INT. CORPORATION STAR SHIP—CARGO BAY— HIGH ANGLE

Across the bay walk TWO MEN.

PULL BACK TO OTS (OVER-THE-SHOULDER)—ALIEN

It watches the men. Drool drips from its lethal jaws.

ALIEN'S POV—THE MEN

It moves in. They react in horror as it attacks. BLOOD SPLASHES, blanking the VP.

CUT TO:

INT. AIRLOCK

The hatch opens and the Alien is ejected by the outward blast of atmosphere. TRACK WITH IT as it flies into space, turning slowly.

V.O.

Ultimately, our limited contact with these creatures indicate that they have simple imperatives that control their lives. They kill, they breed, and they survive.

THE ALIEN

floats in the vacuum. It should be dead by human standards, but it slowly curls itself into a fetal ball, tail wrapped around the massive claw-hammer head and spiky body.

V.O.

Properly utilized, such aliens would make excellent
warriors. Research into their composition could yield
advances in armor, chemical and biological weapons, and perhaps even new ways to induce suspended animation for stellar travel.

PULL BACK—THE ALIEN

Dwindles into a tiny dot, then vanishes altogether
in the cold blackness.

End of script/AV extract. Readers/viewers are once
again warned that unauthorized use of this material
may result in severe penalties, per MILCOM stat.
reg. 342544-A, Revision II.

6

Billie sleeps, but it is not rest. In her dreams she is back on Rim. She sees her parents, sees the inside of the colony that plans to terraform the planet and turn it into paradise. Sees and is happy.

Things blur. Then she sees monsters.

Her life becomes a jumble of hiding, of fear, of waiting for them to find and kill her. She joins the rats under the floor, her mind and actions turn feral. Survival is all, and it is nothing, likely to stop at any moment.

She sees Wilks and the others, guns spraying. She hears the noise, feels the terror.

She feels Wilks's arms around her, feels the vibrations of his weapon as it fires. Watches the monsters shatter and fall, but knows there are too many of them.

There comes the worst moment, when the hard claws of a monster dig into her, lift her, and it carries her away to die. Then it falls, chopped off at the knees. Its blood eats smoking, stinking holes in the floor and it releases her. She doesn't wait, she scrabbles away before it can catch her again. The air is full of acrid fumes, the sound of Wilks's yelling, his gun shooting over and over until it is a continuous roar. The wounded monster's claws click on the floor as it drags itself toward Billie.

She screams. The only name that matters now.

"Wilks!"

The only one who can save her.

7

In the canned-air depths of
MILCOM HQ, in the long hall with invisible doors
two men walked: Orona and Stephens.

"He's as nuts as an orchard full of filbert trees,"
Stephens said. "If we hadn't needed to keep him on
a leash, we'd have psych-DCed him years ago."

"True," Orona said. "But he's what we've got and
GENstaff wants him along. You know how politics
works."

"Yeah, GENstaff thinks he's some kind of monster killer, but I think he's a goddamn *crew* killer."

"You wanted a field command. I got you one."

"Right, carrying Jonah the Jinx into a potentially
lethal force combatsit."

"Let me put it to you like this, Bill," Orona said.
"GENstaff *will* have an experienced person onboard
this project. The only other marine we know about

who has met these things face-to-face and survived
the initial encounter disappeared. The woman and
kid he saved also vanished and we don't know where
they are. The girl Wilks saved is in the bughouse,
doped to the gills. There was also a badly damaged
android, but we don't have a clue as to what happened to it. We're full of mystery here. That leaves
Wilks."

"I don't like it. He's unstable."

"I'm not asking you to *like* it, or like him. I am
telling you that GENstaff says this is how it's going
to be. If you're tired of being a marine, then *you*
call up GENstaff and tell them you don't like it."

Stephens shook his head.

"He's been bumped to sergeant and put in charge
of loading supplies," Orona continued. "How much
damage can he do there?"

Colonel Stephens stood in the loading dock of the
carrier watching the robots haul gear into the ship.
He stopped a private heading for the hydraulic
walkers. "What's in those crates, marine?"

The man snapped to attention. "Sir, plasma rifles
and chargers."

Stephens stared at the hard black plastic boxes.

"Who in the hell authorized plasma weapons?"

"Sir, I don't know, sir. Sergeant Wilks ordered us
to load them, sir. That's all I know, sir."

"As you were."

Stephens took the lift to CARG-OP. He saw Wilks
directing a trio of cargo bots.

"Wilks!"

"Sir."

"Where did you get authorization to requisition plasma weapons?"

"I was ordered to supply the ground troops with appropriate weaponry, sir."

"And you thought blasters were appropriate? We aren't going to war here, Sergeant. We are supposed to collect specimens, not pieces."

"My experience—" Wilks began.

"—has distorted your mind," Stephens finished. "You've taken it upon yourself to provide grossly destructive weaponry when standard-issue carbines will do. That's what you used, wasn't it? And according to your own testimony a 10mm AP would stop one of these things just fine."

Rage flared in Wilks. "First time you face off with these 'things' you'll wish you had something better. Sir."

"GENstaff wants you along, Wilks, so you're along. But I won't jeopardize my mission by splattering potential specimens all over the countryside with weaponry designed to stop tanks. Have those blasters removed from the ship, mister. Is that clear?"

Wilks's voice was ice and steel. "Perfectly clear, Colonel."

The two electroball players darted back and forth inside the hexagonal, walled court, smashing the ball with charged paddles. The fist-sized orb rocketed into multicushioned patterns—three walls were the minimum allowed for a valid point—and came back at the players at over 120 kilometers an hour.

The player on the left executed a perfect six-wall attack. The player on the right was a half second slow in his response and the electroball smashed into his chest hard enough to knock him from his feet.

"Gotcha!"

The hit player came to his feet. "Your point."

"Ready?"

"Go ahead. Serve."

The player on the right smiled. "In a moment. Any news of the merger proposal with Climate Systems?"

Lefty shrugged. "I thought I told you. Our op Massey convinced them to go for it."

The player on the right laughed. "Made them an offer they couldn't refuse, eh?"

"Well. You don't know Massey, but yeah, something like that. Serve."

The two men sat hunched over a holographic table, fingers on the glove pad controls of the electroball game. Inside a clear hexagonal field the miniature players sweated as they darted back and forth, while their operators wore custom and expensive silk business suits and looked considerably fresher. They were well groomed, with ninety-credit hairstyles and precious gem collar studs. They looked very much like corporation vice presidents, which they were.

The tiny ball rocketed off four walls and went past the receiving player.

"Good shot," the man in the vivid green silks said. He wore a ruby the size of his thumb tip at his throat, the red contrasting nicely with the green.

"Yep, almost gave me a decent match," the one in the red silks said. His ornamental throat stud was of diamond, twice the size of his companion's ruby, and it glittered against the red. He was the senior VP of the two.

The hologram shimmered and vanished.

Green Silks said, "Listen, we need to talk about the biowarfare project."

Red nodded. "Anything from the government?"

The two of them stood and moved away from the table. Green said, "Nah, you know how these guys get when they want to keep things secret."

"We need to be in on this," Red said. "We are talking about major credits here. We've had offers from every milsupply corporation in the system if we can come up with the right product. We can't let the military get the jump on us here."

Green smiled. "Don't worry. I'm going to put Massey on it."

They reached a door. It *thwiped* open to admit them into an office the size of a small home. One wall was airglas, giving a view of the megapolis. On a clear day like today, the view was spectacular from eighty stories high. Rank certainly had its privileges.

"Okay, I've been hearing about this guy Massey, but I don't know him. Tell me."

Red moved to a desk big enough to seat five people without crowding.

Green went to a dispenser set into the wall across

from the desk. "Devil dust," he said to the dispenser. "Half a gram. You want anything."

"Yeah, get me an orgy-inhaler."

Green added Red's order to his own. After a second a small tray extruded itself from the machine. On the tray were a small mound of pink powder inside a hemispherical cup set next to a one-shot nasal tube. Green tossed the tube to Red and picked up the cup. He pressed the dust against his left eye as Red fired the compressed gas charge of the inhaler into his right nostril. Both men grinned as the chemicals took hold.

"You were saying about Massey?"

"Oh. Yeah. Him. Well, this guy is something else. MBA from New Harvard, doctorate in corp law from Cornell, post-doc work at Mitsubishi U. Could have had his pick of any company in the system but he *enlisted* in the Colonial Marines. Got a Silver Star in the Oil Wars, four Purple Hearts. Commanded a recon unit in the Tansu Rebellion on Wakahashi's World, picked up a few decorations there."

"Real patriot, huh?" Red said. He squirmed in his chair as another chemically powered orgasm rippled through him.

"Nah. He liked killing. Probably would have gone pretty high up but they court-martialed him. Tried to kill his CO."

"No shit?"

"Yeah. Thought the CO was a coward when he wouldn't order an attack on a bunch of civilians Massey thought might be hiding enemy sympathizers. *Might* be. Knocked the officer senseless and led the attack himself. Killed eighty-five men, women, and children. Word is more than half of them got dispatched by Massey personally."

"Man loved his job, hey?"

"Oh, yeah. We bought the tribunal off and put him to work for us. Good help is so hard to find, you know?"

Green laughed. Red joined him.

Massey sat at the table in his kitchen, his six-year-old son on his lap. Behind him, Marla punched the controls on the coffee maker.

"Be ready in a sec, hon," Marla said. She moved up behind Massey and kissed his neck.

Massey smiled. "Thanks, babe." To his son he said, "So, what's my boy up to today?"

"We're gonna go on a field trip to the zoo," the boy said. "See a Denebian slime spider and maybe the Bartlett snakes, if they'll come out."

"Sounds great," Massey said. He lifted the boy, put him on the floor. "But Daddy's got to go to work now. Say hello to the slime spider for me."

"Oh, Daddy, slime spiders can't talk!"

Massey grinned. "No? What about your uncle Chad?"

Marla swatted at him with one hand. "My brother is not a slime spider!" she said. But she laughed.

"No, that's true," her husband said. "He's only got four limbs, not eight."

"Go, you'll be late for work. Here's your coffee."

Still smiling, Massey left. Yes. Work.

Nothing was more important than work.

Nothing.

Her teeth glittered like stars. They were so beautiful.

Closer she came, magnificent in her huge glory, black and deadly and purposeful. Her exoskeleton gleamed darkly as she leaned down toward Billie. Her mouth opened, and the smaller set of teeth on the inner lips also opened. She was the queen.

I love you, her thoughts came unspoken to Billie. *I need you.*

Yes, Billie thought.

She was the queen, and she reached for Billie, her clawed hands glistening.

Come and . . . join with me, the queen said.

Yes, Billie thought. Yes, I will.

Closer the queen came.

Easley and Bueller squatted behind the remains of the shattered building, a waist-level row of bricks and twisted rebar the only protection against the bunker's R-O-M gun. It couldn't see them but the stupecomp running the gun could probably pick up some heat leakage from their combat suits, and every now and then it would pop off a couple dozen 30mm AP rounds in their direction.

"Shit," Bueller said. "Fucker's got us pinned down!"

"Maybe not," Easley offered. "The thing's got service portals aft. I can launch a grenade in the right spot, it'll blow the power. Then we got his ass."

Three rounds of 30mm clipped a couple of centimeters of brick off the top of the wall over Bueller's head. He squatted lower. "Damn!"

"Okay, look," Easley said, "here's the play. You scoot down about twenty meters, put your weapon over the wall, and spray that sucker. I'll circle around behind it and blow it off line while it's potting at you."

Under the kleersteel faceplate of his helmet cover, Bueller frowned. The expression wrinkled the skintite that reached to his eyes, and the skull of the elite Colonial Marine whack-team embossed on the tite.

"Unless you got a better idea?" Easley said.

Bueller shook his head. "What the hell. Let's do it. Gimme a signal when you're ready to dance."

"Copy," Easley said. His voice was crisp in the helmet's bonephones. The com was standard military tightbeam and scrambled, so the geezer in the bunker couldn't hear them, or even if he could, he wouldn't be able to understand what they were saying.

Bueller moved off, keeping low. Every so often the range-of-motion gun would cap off a few more shots.

Easley lit a low-heat flare and dropped it. With any luck, the gun would think it was a suit leak and zero in on it. While it was doing that, he would blow that sucker. He moved off. He was good, one of the Corps' best, and damned if he was gonna get drilled by some geezer in a lock box.

When he got into position, Easley said, "Do it!"

Thirty meters away, crouched behind a big chunk of rubble that was probably once a house, Bueller whipped his carbine over the top and triggered it full auto. He waved it back and forth, so the motion sensors would get it. The sonics would have found it pretty quick anyhow, but he didn't want to take any chances.

Softsteel slugs spanged off the wall, chopping it away. It knew he was here, all right. Bueller pulled his weapon back so it wouldn't get hit.

Five seconds later, two things happened: a grenade went off and the robotic gun stopped shooting.

Bueller grinned. "Yeah! Way to go, buddy!" Easley must have rammed one right up the thing's drainpipe. Hell of an enema.

Ten seconds went past. "Easley?"

"You're buying the beer tonight, pal," came the reply.

Bueller stood. Oh, man, was *this* sweet! That old fart thought he could play with the best—

A round splashed against Bueller's chest.

"Oh, *shit!*"

He looked down, saw the spatter of phosphorescent green over his heart. If it had been armor-piercing, he'd be history. "Shit, shit, *shit!*"

"You got that right," Wilks said. "How do you do, Mr. Shit." He walked toward Bueller, a training sniper rifle dangling in one hand. Behind Wilks, Easley stood, helmet cover already off, a similar splash of green running down the formerly clear faceplate.

Backing Easley was a squad of marines in field underdress, watching. Wilks wore a synlin coverall and formplast boots.

"You guys stink," he said. "Sure, you sidestepped a few mines and avoided a couple of triplines and you managed to take out a robot gun, but you're still dead meat because you moved stupid."

Behind Wilks, Easley leaned over to the trooper next to him. "You getting this, Blake?"

The second marine, a short blond woman with her hair in the standard combat buzz, nodded. "Yup. Real learning experience. He made you guys look like dung birds."

Easley frowned. "Hey—"

Bueller cut in. "Wait a sec, Sarge. I heard Easley on the tightbeam!"

"No, you didn't. You heard me."

"But—but—that's—that's—"

"Cheating," Wilks finished. "Life is hard. You think these things we're going up against are going to play by some kind of rules?"

Bueller stared at the splotch on his suit.

"So, boys and girls, in honor of this stirring work by Easley and Bueller, we're going to spend the day on the shooting course. Full battle gear, combat scenarios until you can get across without being splashed." Wilks smiled at Bueller, then Easley. "If a wasted old geezer like me can fan two of the CMC's supposedly best whack-teams as easy as I did, the colonies are in a shitload of trouble if they ever need anything worse than a cut skinbonded. Saddle up, marines."

The squad moved off, grumbling.

"—Bueller, you asshole—"

"—damn, Easley, now look what you got us into—"

"—Buddha, you two guys looked like crap—"

Wilks watched them go, pleased. Of course, he

had to rag their asses, that was a TO's job, and since Stephens had busted him out of loading the ship, this was what he could do. But despite his criticism, these guys were good. They'd been to-gether a year, they were all rated high in small arms, explosives, standard strategy and tactics. If he hadn't cheated, he wouldn't have gotten the two hot rods coming at him. They were a lot better than he'd expected. He'd go into enemy fire with this team anytime.

As they pulled armor from the carryall and began to suit up, Wilks remembered his squad on Rim. Were these guys as good as that unit had been? Probably. It was hard to say for sure until things went sour—drill wasn't the same as real, no matter how you tried to make it so. This squad had better scores in training and they moved real well when the return fire was nothing more than splashers. *If* they moved as well in the real world when the bad guys started coming, then, yeah, they would do better than the squad had on Rim.

He hoped to all the gods that they moved better. It was one thing to come up against a nest of the aliens, another thing to be on a planet full of the damned things. And who knew but that their home-world might have worse living on it? Maybe the aliens he'd fought were like mice compared to the worst on their planet. That was a sobering thought. If this team was going to go down and come back, they needed to be good. They needed to be the best. If he could teach them everything he remembered, if he could drill them until they could pointshoot a demicredit out of the air, if he could teach them what they'd be up against . . .

"If" was a big word, even though it didn't look it. There wasn't going to be any room for error in this mission. Screwups would get somebody dead.

And not just dead. The old saying was wrong here: they could kill you and then they *could* eat you. And they would do worse if they took you alive.

The team began to amble back. Wilks brought his thoughts away from what might be to what was. "All right, children, let's see if we can't cross the street without getting run down by a hovercab, shall we? Blake, you take point, Easley, you're TC, Bueller, HW-tactical, Ramirez—"

He finished ordering the squad, then started to give them the scenario. No, he decided. Let them figure it out on the fly. Instead of telling them what they would face, he said, "It'll take forty-five seconds for the holocomp to program the new playing field. That's what you got, people. See if you can't look like marines and not a bunch of turds on legs this time!"

Wilks spoke into his comp-control mike.

Around them the crumbled walls and bunker began to shimmer and dissolve as the computer pulled the plug on the last scenario. Wilks turned and walked away as the obstacle course began to rebuild itself. It would look real and within limits even feel real, but it was an illusion.

What they would be facing when the time came was no illusion. You could spit on that, marine, and damn well make it shine.

8

The conference-room door loomed in front of Billie like the mouth of doom. The conference room in which the review team waited, as it had so many times before.

She took a deep breath and went inside.

Dr. Jerrin stood there, and he wasn't smiling.

Not a good sign.

"Have a seat, Billie," he said.

She looked at the other six faces. Three were doctors she knew, one a medical center administrator, one a legal rep for the government, one her legal rep, the last one here to make sure the usual lynching was all nice and legal.

Billie sat.

Jerrin looked at the other members of the team. He cleared his throat, fiddled with a flat screen on the table. "Ah, Billie, we seem to have come to an . . . impasse in your treatment."

"Really?" Billie said. She couldn't keep the irony out of her voice, but it didn't make any difference. This was only a matter of form. They weren't going to let her out. Not now. Probably not ever. She was going to spend her life in this place.

"Dr. Hannah has suggested a new treatment which, while fairly, ah, dramatic, offers a chance for us to stop these nocturnal episodes of yours."

Billie perked up, but only a little. "Really?" Less sarcasm now.

Jerrin looked at Hannah, a fat blonde from some cold climate, at least to judge by how frigid her words always seemed. Hannah said, "Yes, we've had some success in penal colony treatments with it. It is a fairly simple procedure, an operation using a fine surgical laser that eliminates predefined areas of certain cerebral complexes—"

"What?! You're talking about burning out my brain!"

"Now, Billie," Jerrin began.

"Fuck that! I won't!"

Hannah smiled, a sour expression. "It's not really up to you, dear. The state has certain prerogatives here. You are a danger to yourself and others with your fantasies—"

"They aren't fantasies! Wilks was here, Wilks, the marine who saved me on Rim! Ask him! Find him and ask him!"

She was on her feet now, yelling at Hannah.

The door opened and two orderlies came in, shockers in hand.

"What's she on?" Hannah asked, as if Billie were deaf or not in the room.

Jerrin said, "Triazolam, Haliperidol, Chlorpromazine, double maintenance dose."

"See?" Hannah said. "Habituation. We've rotated her through everything we have and she's used to them all. She shouldn't be able to do much more than walk—and look at her."

Billie struggled in the grip of the two orderlies, able to move them slightly despite their size.

Jerrin sighed. "I suppose you're right."

"Dr. Jerrin! No! Please!"

"It's for the best, Billie. You'll be a lot happier without the dreams."

"But what else will it cost me? Will that be all you take, the dreams?"

Jerrin stared at the table.

"Will it?"

"There may be some slight collateral damage. Minor loss of memory in some areas."

"You fuckers are going to burn who I am away, aren't you? Turn me into a zombie!"

"Now, Billie—"

With a strength born of terror, Billie jerked free of the orderlies and turned to run. She made it to the door before a third orderly slapped her side with his shocker. She fell, unable to control her voluntary muscles.

Oh, God! They were going to wipe her brain. She might as well be dead, because when they were done, there wasn't going to be anybody home.

9

Wilks stared at the computer image as the numbers and words swirled into oblivion. Damn. Had to look, didn't you, Wilks? Had to satisfy your fucking curiosity. Well, now you know.

And now that you do, what are you going to do about it?

Wilks slid out of the form-chair in front of the military terminal. The room was in the MILCOM library complex, normally reserved for officers, but he was a special case, wasn't he? And even if he hadn't been given an emergency clearance to use the system, he could have gotten into the files. You didn't do nineteen years in the Corps without learning a few things.

A few groundpounders sat in booths, working in the stale air as Wilks walked out of the library. It was hard to make rank without combat or offworld

duty at least, and these guys were all cracking the
files, studying, hoping tape-learning education
would give them some kind of edge. He didn't think
it would.

He'd have offered them his spot on the mission in
a San Francisco second, if they wanted to trade, but
that wasn't gonna happen. He was going, unless he
ran, and he couldn't do that. He'd been running
from it too long already.

Okay, pal. You got a look at what you wanted.
Now, what *are* you gonna do about it? Walk away?
You're probably gonna get chewed to soypro a few
hours after you get to the aliens' world. The ship
leaves in eight hours, and you are due to log in in
six. What else can they do to you?

He nodded to himself as he passed a fat major
leaving his studies. The major looked at the chevron
rocker on Wilks's sleeve and frowned. He started to
say something, probably going to rag Wilks about
being in a restricted officers-only area, but Wilks
turned slightly so the man could see the acid burn
scars on his face.

The fat major paled, his hand going involuntarily
to his own blubbery jowls. Wilks could almost see
his mind working. Here was a noncom who wasn't
supposed to be in here and a ranking officer should
check to be sure he had reason and permission. On
the other hand, the noncom in question had a face
like a bad holovee monster program and maybe it
was better just to let him pass. Surely he hadn't
wandered in here by accident, somebody must have
sent him.

Good thinking, fatso, Wilks thought. He smiled, stretching the scar tissue into a grimace.

Okay, fuck it. He was up to here with all this vermin scat. He knew a guy in Programming owed him a big favor. Time to call it in; wasn't like he was going to get to collect old debts much longer anyhow. Might as well go out in style.

Wilks headed to find the man who owed him.

The medical complex loomed like a gleaming and ugly beast of stressed plastecrete and ferrofoam and glass as Wilks left the cab and walked toward it. He had the section, the room number, and a theoretical schedule, courtesy of the programmer in MI-7. Getting off the base hadn't been a problem either, even though he was restricted. For every system they made to do something, there was a way around it. Rank might have its privileges, but the guys on the line knew a few tricks of their own.

The admit pad on the complex door was an old-style keypad, an antique, but that was why he had chosen this entrance, no eye reader. Wilks punched in the code he'd gotten.

The lock chimed and the door slid open. Hell, this was easier than swatting flies. He walked in.

A human guard leaned back in a chair at a desk, looking at porno projection from his handheld vid viewer. He saw Wilks and the naked bodies vanished as he shut the unit down and glanced at his admission roster.

"Can I help you?"

"Yeah, I'm supposed to see Dr. Jerrin."

The guard glanced down. Must have seen Jerrin's

name. He waved his hands over the console, brought up the appointment list. "And you are . . . ?"

"Emile Antoon Khadaji," he said, giving the man a name from an old book he'd once read.

The guard glanced down. "I don't see your name here, Monsieur Khadaji."

Wilks hadn't been able to find and get into the patient file, he hadn't had time, though he had gotten the doctor's name right. "I'm a last-minute deal," he said. "Somebody canceled."

The guard frowned. "I'll have to check with the doctor," he said.

"Fine. Check." He gave the guard a good view of his face. Guy with a face like his surely had psychological problems, right? The guard wasn't suspicious, just following the drill. Probably didn't have a lot to do, he had time to watch porno holos.

As the guard reached for the com unit to call the doctor, Wilks moved his right hand slowly toward his right hip. He had a multicharge pistol, a synapse scrambler, nestled in a flexskin holster on his belt just over his right buttock. He'd gotten the weapon on the black market; it was illegally boosted so it could deliver a stun charge at twice the ten-meter distance for approved civilian hardware.

Wilks looked up and down the hallway. Nobody around.

He pulled the stunner, brought it up, held it in both hands. The heavy plastic felt cool in his grip. It threw a fairly narrow beam, you had to aim it, but he'd had a target laser installed under the stubby barrel. The bright red dot danced over the guard and stopped on his forehead.

The guard looked up. "Hey!"

Wilks shot him.

The guard collapsed in his chair. Wilks moved to arrange him so he looked like he had dozed off. The man would wake up in half an hour with one bitch of a headache, but otherwise should be fine.

He pulled the guard's bar code ID off and clipped it to his shirt pocket. It wouldn't fool a scanner if the thing tried to match his retinal patterns to it, but a human passerby would see that Wilks had a tag and probably think nothing of it. By the time the guard came to, things would be all over, one way or another. But just in case, Wilks bent and fed in the security system lock code virus he'd gotten. The computer terminal digested the code. If it did what it was supposed to do, it would infect the main system in this building. Nobody was going to be calling for outside help from here for a long time, not unless they went to a window and hollered for it. That didn't do anything for internal security, but Wilks figured he could deal with that. He was a Colonial Marine, by all the gods, and the day he couldn't handle some sloppy rent-a-cops, he'd shoot himself. He tucked the stunner back into its holder under his civilian jacket and smiled.

Time to go pick up his date for the prom.

The door to Billie's room slid open. Locked to the bed by the pressor field as she was, she couldn't do more than turn her head slightly.

"Wilks!"

"Yep. Pack your socks, kid. We're going for a ride." He moved to shut the pressor field off.

"How did you—? Why—?"

"We'll talk later," he said. "Right now we need to hustle along. I might have made a couple of enemies on the way in here and I don't think we have time to discuss it."

Billie rolled from the bed. She grabbed a robe and put it on. "I'm ready."

"What, you don't want to fix your hair or spray makeup on or something?" He grinned.

"I'd crawl over broken glass to get out of here. Go."

He turned, stuck his head out into the hall. "Okay. Clear."

She followed him into the hall.

They were doing pretty well until they got to the elevator's atrium. The tube's doors opened and two orderlies and two guards came out, moving fast. The guards had their stunners out and the orderlies both waved shockers.

Wilks never hesitated. He pulled a pistol from under his jacket and fired. Billie watched the little red dot his weapon projected bounce across the heads of the guards and orderlies. Three of them went down, their own weapons clattering quietly on the softfloor. The last orderly, a new one that Billie didn't know, rolled and came up in some kind of martial arts stance, facing Wilks.

Wilks tucked his weapon away. "Stay behind me, kid."

The orderly moved in and swung the shocker like it was a sword.

Wilks dodged to his left, slapped the man's out-stretched arm to one side, and punched him low on the ribs.

The orderly grunted, made as if to turn and swing the shocker again, and Wilks kicked the man, hitting the side of his knee with the edge of his boot.

Billie heard the orderly's knee crack as something gave in it.

The orderly's leg folded and he dropped, but Wilks pulled his foot back and thrust it out again, smashing his heel into the man's head. The orderly flew sideways and slammed into the corridor wall.

"The stairs?"

"That way!"

Billie followed Wilks down the hall to the end. She glanced at the guards and orderlies as she went past. He'd taken them out almost instantly, without even working up a sweat.

"Why didn't you shoot the last one?" she asked as they reached the stairwell.

"Pistol's charge was depleted," he said. "Didn't have time to reload."

They went down two flights—her room was on four—then Wilks led her into the second floor.

"This isn't the ground—" she began.

"I know. They'll have the doors covered by now. We have to find another exit."

She followed him. Two was quiet, and they moved briskly, but not at a run. A tech glanced at them as they passed his station. Wilks smiled and nodded. "How's it going?"

The tech nodded back. Then his control board lit up, pulling his attention away from them.

"Move," Wilks said to Billie. "That'll be the alarm."

Billie ran. There was an emergency escape window at the end of the corridor, but it required a staffer to open it. "That's a coded lock," Billie said.

"Yeah, and I didn't have time to get all the exit numbers," Wilks said. "But I have a nifty little master key, courtesy of the Colonial Marine Corps armory."

Billie found out what he meant as Wilks slapped a wad of what looked like hair gel onto the lock mechanism, squeezed it three times, and waved her back.

Behind them, the tech started yelling. "Hey, you two! Get away from that window! I've called Security!"

The gel flashed bright blue and started to sizzle as if it were a piece of soypro on a too hot grill. The lock's stacked plastic casing bubbled and ran like water.

"Don't look at it," Wilks said. "It'll burn your eyes."

Billie turned to see the tech coming toward them. "Wilks!"

"No problem." He pulled his pistol from under his jacket and pointed it at the tech.

The tech stopped. He held his hands out in front of him defensively. "Hey, hey, take it easy!"

"Get the hell out of here," Wilks said.

The tech turned and ran.

Wilks smiled. "Amazing what even an empty gun can do, ain't it?" He put the weapon away.

The lock dripped into a puddle on the floor, plastic slag. Wilks kicked the window and the unbreakable clearflex swung outward on its side hinges. He leaned out, looked down.

"Too high to jump, we'd break an ankle."

He pulled a small device from under his jacket. Billie watched as he unfolded a pair of handles that jutted at right angles from the thing, a rounded square of black plastic the size of a big man's hand.

Wilks pointed the device at the windowsill and touched a control on it. It popped loudly. A thin line of white sprayed out from a nozzle on the end and hit the sill. He touched another control and loops of the line paid out. "One, two, three, four," he said. "Okay, it's set. Climb onto my back," he said.

Billie obeyed.

With that, he stepped up onto the sill, turned to face the hallway, and began to climb down the outside wall. The line coming out of the thing in his hands looked awful thin to support them. He said, "Hang on, I'm going to lean back."

She clutched him tightly with her arms and legs. Holding them with his arms outstretched, he began to walk backward down the wall.

"Spider gear," he said. "Don't worry, this line'll support ten men without breaking."

It took no more than a few seconds for them to reach the ground.

As she slid from his back, Billie said, "Where are we going?"

"Does it matter?"

She shook her head. No. It didn't matter. Anywhere was better than having her brain diced and scrambled.

The pair of them hurried away.

10

"This is Salvaje, bringing you word of the True Messiah. Listen to me, my fellow seekers.

"I know that which you lack.

"I know of your incompleteness.

"I have the answer.

"The True Messiah can make you into a Holy Receptacle. For it is in bearing the sons and daughters of the Messiah that you will find your salvation. Listen, and know that I speak only the truth! False prophets and false gods have brought our world to the brink of ruination! False gods ask that you worship them from afar, but they remain cold and aloof and sterile. The True Messiah will join with you! You can feel the True Messiah, touch the True Messiah, become one with the True Messiah! Do not allow yourselves to be misled any longer, my brothers and sisters! Throw off the chains and shackles of your oppression, get rid of the old and make room in yourself for the new!

"The True Messiah is coming, brothers and sisters. Soon the communion will be possible, and only those who open themselves to the ultimate experience will survive the coming devastation that man has brought upon himself! Prepare, prepare yourselves for the Coming! Listen for the call in your dreams! Listen and heed!"

"That's it, doc," Pindar said. "We're off the air."

Salvaje shrugged. "Install a new dish. My message must continue to go forth."

It was Pindar's turn to shrug. "It's your money."

"Money means nothing, fool. My parents left me millions, the faithful send me millions more. Soon it will be worthless, as all the works of man will become worthless on this fouled planet. The True Messiah is coming. Soon."

Yeah, right, Pindar thought. Maybe he should take some of Salvaje's about-to-be-worthless credits and spend a couple of days in Madam Lu's Pleasure House. Long as the Messiah was coming, no reason why Pindar couldn't come a little himself.

"Anything you say," Pindar said. What a shamoo this guy was. Crazy as a stepped-on roach. But as long as he paid, what the hell. He could dance naked in peanut butter for all Pindar cared. Two more like him and he could retire.

True Messiah. Yeah. Right.

11

Green and Red came out of the theater where their limo idled, fanning up grit from the street-level plastecrete road. The driver touched a control and the rear door slid up. Green and Red entered the limo and sank into form-cushions whose machineries adjusted to fit them perfectly. "To the tower," Red ordered the driver.

The limo lifted slightly and slid away on its cushion of air.

"What did you think?" Green asked.

"Did people really used to go out to gather and listen to noise like that?"

Green laughed. "So the history books say. Rock concerts, they called them. Actually attending them instead of sitting comfortably in their own living rooms and watching it on the holovee."

"What was the point?"

"It was for the totality of it—sight, sound, smells, feelings—a shared experience."

Red shook his head. "A wonder we ever got civilized. Risking death on the unregulated roadways to listen to that jarring shit. Also a wonder they all weren't deaf."

"Hey, times change. We don't wear animal skins and hit each other over the head with clubs anymore, either."

"Speaking of clubs . . . how is the intercept going?"

"As well as could be expected."

"That business with whatshisname? Massey? No problems there?"

Green nodded. "No. It's been resolved."

"What exactly happened? I didn't get the full details."

Green reached over to the limo's bar and punched in a code. After a moment, the dispenser delivered two bulbs of some frothy blue liquid. Green took one, handed the second to Red. "Ah. Not bad for a robot bar."

"You were saying . . . ?"

"Ah, yes. Well, one of the communications people slipped up. Sent an uncoded file to Massey's residence. Computer didn't catch it. Real snafu. That would have been bad enough, but unfortunately, Massey's son accessed the material."

"Stupid," Red said, sipping at his drink.

"Extremely so. The boy showed it to his mother. Neither of them understood the full implications, of course, but they got enough of it to possibly compromise the mission. Massey was in the shower when the message came through. When he got out, his wife started babbling about what they'd seen." Green squirted more of the froth into his mouth. "Massey really had no choice, not if he wanted to maintain security."

The boy smiled at his father. Massey returned the smile. Reached out and took his son's head gently in his hands. The move was so fast the boy didn't have time to be surprised. A hard twist. The snap of bone, the instant limpness.

His wife's eyes widened in horror, but before she could even begin to digest the impact of what she had seen, Massey reached her. A single, practiced move, fast, no suffering. It had to be done, but he had grown fond of them, after all. It was the best he could do. They deserved that much.

"God. That's cold," Red said.

"Yes. It was SOP, of course, but they had been married for six years. Even as cover, you'd think he'd want somebody else to do the wetwork on this one. But he did it himself. The company made sure the investigative team from the local police were friendlies and Massey's story about coming home to find them dead was accepted. The local law figures it as a robbery gone bad or a wilding by somebody clever enough to bypass building security."

"What about the communications tech, wasn't there something about that?"

Green finished his bulb, punched up another one. Looked at Red with one eybrow raised.

"No, I'm fine."

Green said, "Massey took him out. Fed the body into an industrial disposal unit that makes fertilizer. Guy is probably helping flowers and vegetables grow in half a dozen countries by now."

"Pissed Massey off, I imagine."

"Well, that's the strange thing. Not personally. Massey killed him cleanly, no torture or anything, if what I heard is correct. It was just another job to him."

"Buddha, that *is* cold. Guy was responsible for the death of my spouse and kid, I'd want him to twist a little in the breeze before I finished him."

"Yeah, but you aren't a sociopath. With Massey, the job is what comes first, last, and always. He doesn't care what he has to do to get it done."

Red pretended to shiver. "We got some kind of failsafe on this guy?"

"Of course. You don't think we'd let a man like that run around without a control, do you? He's got a cap of C9 circset into his hypothalmus, along with a beeper. He ever turns on us, somebody in Security only has to get within a klick of him and send a coded pulse—and blammo! Massey's head turns into a big bowl full of mushy brain salad."

"Good," Red said. "Guys like him are necessary, but I'll sleep better knowing we can take him out if need be."

"Not to worry," Green said. "It's our job to think of these things. We've got it covered."

Massey left the funeral of his wife and son, looking somber but playing a role. He didn't feel anything in particular about the loss. One less woman and child didn't mean anything, and while it was true he'd gotten used to them, he'd get used to them being gone, too. That's how it was.

Behind him, his control dogged his heels, blending skillfully into the passersby outside the crematorium. The man was good, but Massey had spotted him months ago. He hadn't let on, of course, because it was better to have the devil you knew tailing you than the one you didn't know.

Massey wanted to grin, but he kept his face neutral as he caught a walk moving down from the crematorium level toward the elevated p-mover that would take him home. The company thought it was real clever, injecting a bioexplosive into his system during a routine physical. Massey had more money than he knew what to do with, and with enough credits, you could get a very good doctor. The C9 had been easy enough to remove. The pinhead-sized capsule had also been easy to load into a high-pressure injector gun. When Massey had taken his "vacation" to the Amazon Preserve a few weeks ago, they'd followed him, of course. The Preserve was almost twenty square kilometers of "authentic" rain forest, bounded by high containment fields that kept the animals in and civilization out. Local wildlife included such pests as insects, some of which liked to bite. Massey's control had lost his insect repellent, or so he'd thought, and when the mosquitoes began eating at him, one of them had bitten him particularly hard. He'd slapped his hand over the wound but missed the flying bug. Because that particular bite wasn't from an insect at all.

And now, that deadly C9 capsule was lodged in

the control's brain. The day he sent a coded pulse to kill Massey would be most surprising. And, Massey thought, particularly fitting. He'd kept the locator they'd put in, slightly altered. He didn't give a damn if they knew where he was for now. When he decided he didn't want them to know anymore, the beeper would stop sending its signal as quickly as he could touch a button on his belt.

The doctor who'd performed the surgery was now part of a batch of steel forming a bridge suspension on Mars, if Massey's information was correct. No loose ends to tangle things.

As long as they let him do his job, Massey wouldn't have any problems with the company. But if they somehow lost faith, well, there was no point in being unprepared. Mistakes happened, even though he didn't make them. Always better to be ready than not.

The job this time was a big one, worth a lot of credits. For him the money was just a way to keep score. So far, Massey was winning big. There wasn't anybody else close. The company thought it was clever, but they didn't belong in the same class with him. He was the best. He intended to keep on being the best for a long, long time.

While Wilks was only a sergeant and theoretically subject to command by any officer of line rank, the truth of it was that on this mission, only Stephens was going to be giving him orders. They wanted him on this ship and so they'd bent over and handed him the soap. Wilks figured he might as well use it.

The first thing he did was program the ship's

computer with a personal override, using the last bit of the favor he was owed. He could come and go pretty much as he wanted. Getting Billie on the ship was easier than getting her out of the medical center. When Wilks accompanied two of the spare hypersleep chambers into the loading bay, Billie was inside one of them, the lid opaqued. Nobody even bothered to question him; he waltzed past the trooper leaning against the door with nothing more than a few words.

"Hey, Sarge," the man said. "You cuttin' it kinda thin, ain'tcha? It's only five minutes to log-on dead-line."

"Live fast, die young—" he began.

"—and leave a good-looking corpse," the trooper finished. He laughed.

Wilks shook his head. A lot of civilians believed that Colonial Marines were all steely-eyed, boot-tough, deadly as a box full of Acturian wasps and as sharp as a room full of needles. The entertainment vids made it out that little, if anything, got past a trained marine. That they could chew up nails and pee thumbtacks. The truth was that a basic trooper was usually a kid, barely old enough to be depilating his peach-fuzz whiskers, and as big a sucker as any teenager. It didn't take a genius to pass basic military entrance exams. If you could find your way to the test site and spell your name for the computer, you were probably bright enough to get in. How long you stayed alive after that depended on how well the training took and how stupid your officers were, but the myth of the take-charge marines was just that, a myth.

Wilks walked the chambers past the trooper, floating them easily on their humming repulsors. Nobody expected anybody to smuggle a person onto a military ship *leaving* Earth. Coming back, maybe, a lot of folks wanted to get home out in the frontier worlds, but few people wanted to go bad enough to sneak into an outbound ship.

Stephens would shit a square brick when he found out, but by then it would be too late. You weren't gonna turn a star hopper around and make a fifty-light-year run back to Earth to drop off a stowaway. And on this mission, you weren't going to take any side trips along the way, either. Hell, they were going to be gone more than a year in realtime, exactly how long was classified, time they got back all kinds of things could have changed.

Wilks shrugged. Stephens was an idiot. A desk rider, no field experience at all, much less in combat. He must have pulled in some chits to get this assignment, and he didn't have the least idea of how dangerous it was. Jerking the plasma weapons was his first stupid mistake. He just wanted to show Wilks who was in command. Well. He'd live to regret it. Probably they'd all live to regret it.

Wilks jockied the chambers into the sleep compartment. He touched a button and the lid on Billie's fanned up.

"Okay, kid, here's what's happening. We're going to go to the monsters' planet. You and I, we know how these things are, but nobody believes us. Probably we won't be coming back."

Her face went white.

"I can still off-load you, you want."

A long moment hung suspended between them. Finally, she shook her head. "I've lived with them most of my life," she said. "Might as well face them and get it over with, one way or the other."

He nodded. "That's about how I see it. All right. I'm going to run the lines into this unit and put you to sleep. See you on the other end."

"Yeah."

He started to close the lid.

"Hey, Wilks?"

"Yeah?"

"Thanks for coming to get me."

He shrugged. "We got something in common, kid. We both should have died on Rim."

She nodded. "Yes. I know."

"Maybe we can kick some bug-ass before we go."

She nodded again. "I'll keep that thought."

"I hope you don't dream, kid."

"You, too."

He shut the unit and moved it into place. It only took a few seconds to attach the cryo lines and power supply. He triggered the unit and set the timer.

"Sleep well, kid."

With that, Wilks turned and walked away.

12

DATA SCAN—SINGLE READ-
ING ONLY

:. :: ..: ..: ...:: ...:... :::.. . ....: . . . ..::::.::

Authorized Personnel, REQUIRED CLEARANCE
TS-1. Bionational Internal Memorandum 385769.1/
A, rev. II

Operation Outreach

Progress Report:

Government vessel *Benedict* lifted as scheduled
April 5, 2092 0900, Toowoomba Military Launch
Pad. Standard ship crew, plus Squads 1–4, Fox
Platoon, Company Able, 1st. Extee Division, Sec-
ond Colonial Marines. Colonel H. S. Stephens,
Commanding. (See attached, personnel appendix,
A.)

Bionational ship K-014 launched in pursuit,
echo-lock, 4/5/92, 0900.5, full robotics & expend-

able EXP-series android crew under the command
of Executive Assistant, Security, P. Massey.

(Joel—You know the general layout of this, but
I'll recap some of the particulars you might have
missed while you were on vacation. The alien life
form the guv guys want is the big nasty, and
naturally they'd like to score it for their own weapons program. Needless to say this would compromise our own profit structure were it to happen.
With the recent Supreme Court decision on patent-
able life forms, vis-à-vis created versus discovered,
we might spend ten years in the fucking legal
system trying to unsnarl this mess. So up-levels
decided that we should tail the feds to the homeworld [the location of which is so damned secret we
couldn't pry it out of anybody for blackmail or
money] and get as much info as we could.

And, of course, we don't want the feds to get their
own specimen. This guy Massey has his orders and
he's the best there is—he will do *what*ever it takes
to stop them.

You probably have heard that Research got its
hands on a guy salvaged from a cargo express, one
of ours, fortunately, with one of the big nasty embryos wrapped around his face. The ship was cold,
systems dead, but somehow this thing had kept
him in stasis, almost as if he'd been in a sleep tank.
Hell, that alone is worth a fortune if we can figure
out how the hell it did it.

Anyway, both the crewman and the bug on his
face were still alive, so they've been brought to the
Houston labs for analysis. We're still way ahead of
the feds on this, and already geared up for full-scale

testing. Start figuring out ways to spend your bonus, Joel, we're all going to get rich off this one. That's it on the main deal. There's some other stuff in this memo the psycho boys are concerned about, so I'll let you get to it. See you for lunch Tuesday—Ben.)

FILE EXCERPT—MEDICAL—Case #23325 —Maria Gonzales

Patient is a 24 y/o unmarried WD, WN female Caucasian Hispanic, gravida 0, complaining of nightmares. Physical examination unremarkable, no known allergies, PH of illness limited to minor URIs, occasional general malaise, broken L. fibula, age 09. Laboratory workups, including SMA-60, CBC, urinalysis, CAT scan, all within normal limits. Patient has ten-year BC implant, no other medications.

DR. RANIER: Maria, tell me about the dream.

GONZALES: Okay, okay, I'm ridin' on the subway in L.A. with my mother—

RANIER: Your mother died several years ago?

GONZALES: *Sí*, cancer. (pause) We're on the Wilshire tube going into downtown and the tube is empty except for us. (pause—laugh) That's the really scary part, you know? I never seen an empty subway car.

RANIER: Go on.

GONZALES: So all of a sudden there is this loud noise, like something hits the roof of the subway. Then a scraping sound.

RANIER: Scraping?

GONZALES: (agitated) Yeah, like something digging, you know? But it's also like fingernails on metal. (pause) [Examiner's Note: Patient exhibits increasing nervousness, marked diaphoresis, pallor.]

Anyway, then the train stops and I realize that something is trying to get in. Something bad. So I say to my mother, Mama, come on, we have to get out of here! But Mama, she just sits there and smiles at me, you know? (pause)

Then all of a sudden the roof tears open like it's paper and these *things* claw right into the car. Like nothing I've ever seen, they are *bestia, como se dice*? monsters, with teeth and big heads like bananas. I reach for Mama to pull her with me, only she turns into one of the things, her face stretches! It is too horrible! And it feels so . . . real.

Case #232337—Thomas Culp

DR. MORGAN: What happened after the holovee came on?

CULP: Well, the room looked distorted, twisted, somehow. (pause) Then something like, came out of the set, but it stretched the usual stopping place of the holograms. Like a fist shoving through a sheet of flexiplast. And then the thing—some kind of monster—it grabbed me. I couldn't move a fucking muscle! It opened its mouth, had teeth as long as my fingers, and inside was like another mouth, smaller, and it opened, and, oh, Buddha! It *got* me and I couldn't fucking move!

Case #232558—T. M. Duncan

DUNCAN: So I was standing next to the flight attendant, hitting on her a little, and then I noticed she looked familiar, like somebody I knew.

DR. FRANKEL: Familiar? Did you recognize her?

DUNCAN: Yeah, it took a second. She looked like my mother. So I figure, well, I shouldn't be trying to come on to my mother, then all of a sudden, her chest tore open and this thing looked like a snake or a big eel with a lot of teeth comes out, spewing blood and all and flew, fucking *flew* out of her right at my face! (pause) That's when I woke up, and man, I was never so glad in my life to be awake. I stayed up for two days.

Case #232745—C. Lockwood
LOCKWOOD: It was wet, slick with blood, shiny, hard, like some kind of giant dick with teeth and it wanted to jam itself into me!

In his office, Orona waved his computer to hold and turned to his assistant. "Interesting. All from within a fifty-klick area, you said?"

"Yessir. And the medicomp has collected a dozen other similar reports."

"What have the patients in common?"

"High ratings on the Cryer Scale and at least double digits on the Emerson Empathic."

"Ah. And the descriptions are identical?"

"Virtually identical."

"Etiology?"

"Unknown. Best guess the medicomp can come

up with is some kind of telepathic or empathic projection. Perhaps it is how the things communicate among themselves and perhaps they are trying to communicate with us."

"Hmm," Orona said. He frowned. "Our data so far do not indicate that the aliens are particularly intelligent, per se. And we've kept a pretty tight lid on this thing. And yet here we are having a wave of spontaneous . . . connections of some kind. Why now? And why here on Earth? There aren't any aliens here."

The computer readout over the bed carried a full-ride telemetry chart. The patient, Likowski, James T., lay in the pressor grip of a state-of-the-art Hyperdyne Systems Model 244-2 Diagnoster. His EEG, ECG, myotonous level, basal metabolic rate, systems mitosis rates, and full blood counts flowed in continuous waves, words, and patterns across the monitor. Blood pressure, respiration, and pulse rate were noted and logged. The diagnoster checked and corrected the temperature so the patient was not too cold nor too hot. The IV shunt in his left femoral vein fed him the perfect liquid mix of nutrients for optimum health. An indwelling Foley catheter and rectal drain carried away wastes. The company had spared no expense when it came to taking care of this particular patient. The clean room was under Full Isolation Technique, and all visitors, medical or corporate, wore full osmotic surgical suits with their own air supply. The south wall was mirrored one-way, and observers could see the patient directly through the triple-paned glass should they choose. Seven doctors formed the main care team, with six medical technicians working in shifts as monitors, plus eighteen guards and a Full Alert status for the entire wing of the mediplex. Likowski, James T., was not going anywhere, nor was anybody not cleared coming to see him.

Two men stood in the observation room, watching the patient. One was tall, fair, almost bald, and brilliant. He was Tobias Dryner, M.D., T.A.S., Ph.D., and the team leader. The other man was shorter, darker, hairier, and not quite so smart, but hardly stupid. He was Louis Reine, also M.D., T.A.S., but without the extra doctorate in biosystems. Still, he was a company man and a vice president in the Biomed Division, which counted for a lot. Dryner was in charge of the patient, but Reine was in charge of the project.

"How is he?" Reine asked.

Dryner waved his hand over a motion-sensitive control. "Listen for yourself."

The audio came on: "—somebody tell me what the hell is going on? What happened? I want to talk to my wife. Goddammit, why am I here? I feel fine! Just a little stomachache is all, I don't need all this crap!"

Dryner waved his hand again and the sound faded. He moved to a Magnetoencephalo axial holographic viewer away from the glass wall and stroked a control. The screens lit with the MAH scan, showing a man at quarter-scale. The image blurred, shifted, and the skin and overlying muscles faded to show the internal organs. The image began to rotate slowly on its axis. Dryner touched another control. Under the man's ribs, inside the stomach, the alien fetus glowed a computer-enhanced green.

"Give me a full size on the CE image," Dryner ordered.

The alien grew fourfold.

"Interesting," Reine said, watching as the image turned. "No wonder he has a stomachache."

"It is drawing small amounts of blood from a minor artery, here," Dryner said, pointing at the image with one finger. "Otherwise, it's not damaging him. The rate of growth is phenomenal. If this were a human baby, it would come to term in a matter of days, not months. The physiology is impossible; it can't be getting enough nourishment from him. Must be consuming stores of some kind, either that or one devil of a miraculous metabolic system."

"Looks something like a kidney bean with teeth," Reine observed. "Ugly bastard." A pause. "Does the pilot know it's in there?"

"As such, no. He feels a certain amount of discomfort. We have done a neural stimulation to up his own endorphin and enkephalin levels so he isn't feeling pain, merely pressure. We didn't want to risk drugging the parasite with something that might harm its system."

"Good idea."

"Of course, there are some ethical questions as to whether we should inform the patient, given the ultimate prognosis."

"Your opinion?"

"Well, we are studying a new life form. Behavior of the host organism could be important. Perhaps certain hormonal secretions would be altered if the patient knew. The effect of such changes on the parasite could be detrimental or beneficial—it is hard to say. Offhand, the Chemistry boys guess that an increase in epinephrine would probably accelerate the thing's growth."

"You mean that if he knows the thing is going to chew its way out and kill him when it comes to term he'd probably be scared shitless and the bug would like that?"

"It is possible."

Reine sighed. "This thing could be worth *billions*, you know that? And the pilot is living on borrowed time. He has family?"

"A wife and two children."

"They'll get the company policy?"

"Of course."

"Then tell him."

Red wadded up the hard-copy security fax and tossed it in a hook shot at the disposal unit. The thin sheet of plastic hit the field as it fell toward the mouth of the unit and vaporized with a yellow flash and a thin *pop!*

The door to the office opened and Green entered. The two men smiled at each other. Green said, "Read the fax from Houston?"

"Oh, yeah."

"I put out a few rumors, very hush-hush. Quan Chu Lin's people practically came all over themselves to make offers. He's willing to give us top credit for an exclusive if this pans out even half as good as I painted it."

Red snickered. "His ass. We can bootstrap this sucker up so high that Quan Chu's money will look like pocket lint."

"That's what I figured. But it doesn't hurt to bait the waters a little. Get the sharks all roiled up and ready to bite each other for a taste of what we can feed 'em."

"Right about that, pal. I'm already shopping for a house on Maui. Maybe I'll buy myself a ship and do the Belt next summer, what do you think?"

Green laughed. "Why not? You'll be able to afford it. Me, I'm thinking about getting one of the new Hyperdyne 129-4s—the love slave model."

"A pleasure droid? Nice. If your wife will let you."

"What the hell, maybe I'll get her one, too. That way she'll be so busy, she won't even notice I'm gone."

Both men laughed. If this went the way it should, it would be as good as winning the lottery. At least.

13

Salvaje lay on the whore's bed, watching the naked woman hang panties on the line strung across the end of the room. The apartment was a basic-dole unit in a high rise and the hot wind from the open window rose from the floors below, carrying with it the stench of too many people crammed into too small a space. Cooked vegetables and sweat and broken toilets added their odors to the stink.

The naked whore was pregnant, seven months along, at least, and carrying a hefty fetus from her look. Her implant had failed and she'd decided to have the baby. There was a nice market for healthy ones; people came down from the north who wanted a newborn without having to bear it themselves. She could get six months pay, easy. Besides, she knew there were some men who found something appealing about pregnant women. Not what he found appealing, but something.

Salvaje stared at her, an eagle watching a tasty mouse.

The whore finished hanging her underwear up. She turned toward him. He was also naked.

"*Dios,* is that all you gonna do, is watch me? You don' wan' to, you know, let me *do* something for you?" She formed a circle with her hand and moved it as a man would if masturbating. Then she touched her lips with a fingertip, her pubic hair with the other hand.

"No," he said. "I want to watch you. And I want you to tell me about how it feels to have a life inside of you."

The whore shrugged. "It's your money."

"Yes, it is. Come here."

She moved toward him on the bed, sat. He put one hand on her belly, under a pendulous breast. "You know the miracle of carrying life," he said. "It must be wonderful."

She laughed. "Oh, yeah, it's won'erful, okay. My back hurts, my feet swell all up, I got to go pee twelve, fifteen times a day and night. The baby kicks me so hard it almost knocks my pants off sometimes. Won'erful."

"Tell me more," he said. He felt himself stirring. Yes. She carried nothing more than a bastard whose father was a paying customer—he doubted the whore even knew or cared who had put it into her— but even so, she was closer to *knowing* than he was. He envied her, and until the Messiah arrived, this was as close as he could come to finding out how it felt.

She grinned at his erection. "Ah," she said, misunderstanding. "You want to know what it's like, okay, I tell you. I make it good for you. The best."

Later, as Salvaje reached the door to his own apartment, Pindar the technician slogged through the rain toward him.

"Where have you been, I've been waiting here almost a fucking hour!"

"I'll pay you for your time, don't worry."

"My time is exactly what I *am* worried about," Pindar said. "Like, where I am going to be spending it if I get caught doing this? You are getting kind of famous, you know. The G-boys have a monitoring team working to find you. Something is going on, something more than the usual sweep for somebody doing pirate 'casts. What are you into, here, Salvaje?"

Salvaje opened the door and the two of them moved in out of the rain. "They fear me," he said. "Because of my message."

"Ratshit," Pindar said. "There are a hundred like you breaking into the nets every day. They preach about everything from pure water to group sex being the way to God. The TCC doesn't work up a sweat trying to run them down, but somehow *you* rate a full-scale investigation. They want you bad. I have been questioned."

"And you told them . . . ?"

"Nothing, you think I'm stupid? They can bury a man so deep nobody can find him again. But I want

to know what I'm into here. Why are you so important?"

"I told you, my message."

"Listen—"

"No, *you* listen! You are nothing, you are an
insect! The Messiah is coming! I am a tool of the
incarnate god and I will not be slowed by such as
you. If you need something to fear, then fear me,
technician. I have eyes and ears everywhere, and if
you fail to serve me, there will be no hole deep
enough to hide you from my retribution, do you
understand?"

Pindar shook his head and started to turn away.

Salvaje grabbed him by the shoulders, spun him
around, and shoved him so hard the man fairly flew
backward to slam into the wall.

"Fuck!"

"If you do anything to thwart my broadcasts I will
see to it that you die in a way more horrible than
anything you can possibly imagine! Do you understand?"

The technician's eyes went wide with sudden
fear. "Yeah, yeah, okay, okay! It's just getting dangerous, that's all I wanted to say. It'll cost—"

"I care not what it costs! The time is almost upon
us. The message must continue. My organization is
formed, I have hundreds, thousands, who do my
bidding without knowing who I am, but I need the
message to go forth!"

Pindar stared at Salvaje. Salvaje felt nothing but
contempt for the technician. He was weak, cow-
ardly, fearing of things that had no meaning. The

Messiah would have no use for such as this. None
at all.

Onboard the Bionational ship K-014 somewhere
in the nowhen and nowhere of hypershift, Massey
spoke to his crew of androids. They were experimental models with short lifespans and were definitely expendable. The company had made up just
this one batch with their particular modifications,
and if word got out how they'd been altered, the
company would have to do some fast singing and
dancing to explain it. The androids could have been
programmed with the mission before leaving Earth,
but Massey was not one to take chances. By keeping
it to himself, risk was minimized. You couldn't pry
an answer from somebody who didn't have it, and
Massey could snuff his own life if he were ever
captured, leaving only questions.

Massey stood in front of the holographic wall,
images of the government transport ship *Benedict*
floating just behind him. "All right," he said, "here
is our target. There are five main entrances, three
emergency hatches, nine service portals, counting
the main bay. Our primary entrance will be the
number one aft hatch, here." He pointed at
the shimmering image. "Secondary entrance, in
the event of blockage, will be the number two
forward hatch here. Tertiary entrance will be the
number one emergency hatch, here."

The androids watched, not speaking.

"You will be armed with splatterguns for soft
targets only. While these are trained marines, we
will have surprise on our side—they are not expect-

ing us. Plus we have other ammunition in our arsenal.

"The crew and marine survivors will be kept alive until we reach our destination, where we will likely have further use for them. Access the tactical computer for your individual assignments, full data base assimilation by 0400 tomorrow. That's all."

The android crew sat, still unspeaking. They were, Massey knew, up to the task. There was some risk of failure, a tang of spice, as it were, but Massey did not doubt that he could overcome the slight chance. He had worked out the plan in the finest details, he had covered everything. He was the best there was at this kind of thing, and he would succeed. That was the point, really. Not the money he was paid, not the fortunes the company would make, not the deaths of the androids or the other crew. The thing was, as always, the challenge.

This was perhaps the trickiest job he had ever taken on, and he intended that it come out as smooth as machine lube on polished crystal. Massey had but one goal, the same as it had always been: to win. Anything less would not do. Better to die than to lose.

He grinned. He wasn't ready to die yet. So he wouldn't.

Onboard the transport ship *Benedict* when the marines came out of hypersleep, the surprise took a while to filter through to Stephens. Wilks wondered if the man would have noticed at all had not the head count come out one too many.

The squads picked it up right away—they all

knew each other—so Billie stood out for them. But
Stephens was a chair jockey; he had a list of his
troops somewhere and couldn't yet identify them
by names or faces.

Wilks watched the colonel frown at the numbers
on his flat screen.

"Sergeant Wilks," Stephens said.

"Sir."

"I've got a plus-one on my roster."

Wilks thought about letting it slide, just to see,
but he'd find out sooner or later. No point in putting
it off forever. "Yes, sir. I brought an extra person,
sir."

Stephens blinked as if still groggy from the
chamber. "What?"

"Sir. A civilian expert on the aliens."

"What?! Are you crazy? This is a top-secret military mission, Sergeant! I'll have your butt court-
martialed! They'll put you in a pit so deep it'll take
the ceiling light a year to get to you!"

Wilks could feel some of the marines smiling, but
he didn't look to see which ones. He said, "Yes, sir."

Stephens looked at the troopers, and Wilks knew
he was trying to figure out which one he didn't
know. Trying and failing. He stalled. "I told them
you were unreliable. You could have screwed up this
entire mission, mister! G-ship balances are critical
at light-year jumps! An extra person could have
thrown us a parsec off while in hypershift!"

"I balanced the weight, sir. I dumped fifty kilos
of that raspberry-flavored shit from stores just prior
to lift off."

Behind Wilks, Bueller whispered to Easley: "Too bad. I liked that raspberry-flavored shit myself—"

"Shut up," Easley whispered back.

"I am going to throw you in the brig and scramble the code," Stephens said, still looking for who didn't belong. Since they were all still in robes over their sleeptites, there was nothing to give Billie away; a robe also covered her hospital clothes. As stupid as it was, Wilks was amused that Stephens couldn't make her. Confirmed his opinion of the colonel.

Time to flex a little muscle. "Sir, you could do that. But perhaps GENstaff might be interested in knowing why the CO didn't discover the stowaway before lift-off, given that a final inspection is part of the CO's duties. Sir."

Wilks knew this was Stephens's first field command and that he did not want anything to mar it, make him look bad. Now was the time for his pitch. "Sir, if I might have a more private word?"

Stephens was pissed, no doubt about it, but he had to be working the angles, trying to see how this was going to look once he got home. Since Wilks wouldn't bet a bent demicred that he was going to get home, that didn't much matter to him, but Stephens wouldn't be thinking like that.

Stephens turned and moved toward the aft wall.

Wilks followed him. Behind them, the squads stood at parade rest, watching and trying to hear.

When they were far enough away, Stephens turned. His fury was unabated. "This better be goddamned good, Wilks."

"Sir, if you could show that *you* were responsible for taking on a civilian expert, then there wouldn't be any problem. You buried a CMA code in your log, didn't you?"

Stephens glared at Wilks. If eyes were lasers, Wilks would have been a crisp brown spot sizzling on the deck by now. Wilks hadn't been able to check Stephens's CO log, the access commands for that were beyond his abilities as a computer break-in artist, but he was fairly certain that the colonel had installed a CMA—cover my ass—code so that it was dated near the start of the mission. This was SOP among nervous officers, a simple piece of insurance that could sit there unused, unless something wonky came up. It was easy enough. Log entries were all automatically timed and dated; a CMA code was some innocuous piece of input, usually a phrase that was related to whatever data were going in, but stilted in such a way that it didn't quite fit. If a situation arose that was unforeseen, the officer could use the code to cover himself by entering new data and then referring back to the phrase, as if it had been put there in anticipation of such happenings. Any lengthy phrase could be made to say almost anything a bright computer wanted later, and the officer could swear he or she had known about it in advance and covered it, but in code, so as to keep it secret from prying eyes.

Suppose your cook was stealing supplies and selling them on the black market. You came up a couple hundred kilos short when you did inventory. This would make a CO look bad. But if there was a code that said something like "Suspect that cook is stealing supplies, will allow him to continue to build case," then you knew you were on top of it, and what you did was justified in the interests of being certain. It was an old trick, one that shouldn't fool anybody who'd been in the service more than ten minutes, but one bad officers still used. Wilks was certain Stephens would have done it.

"Why should I help you?"

"Because, sir, you'd be helping yourself. I'll put the rumor out that our . . . discussion here is part of a clever subterfuge you worked up, for reasons of your own having to do with some kind of secret military business about which they don't want to know. When we get back to Earth, you're covered and I'll go quietly wherever you want me to go."

Stephens considered it. He didn't like it, Wilks could see that, but he was thinking about his future and that was the most important thing on his agenda. "All right," he said. "Trot him out and let me see him."

"See her," Wilks said.

"Where did you get her?"

"I broke her out of a mental hospital. Sir."

14

Wilks sat next to Billie in the mess hall as they picked at the reconstituted eggs and hard biscuits of the microwaved Ship Meal Packet. Billie had eaten worse, but not recently.

"You okay, kid?"

She nodded. "Yeah. A few aches and stiffness, but otherwise all right."

Wilks ate a bite of his too yellow scrambled eggs. As he did, Billie glanced around the room. First squad sat bunched in twos or threes at tables nearby. There were eight of them, and Billie had made a point of matching the names and faces within a few hours of awakening. Five men and three women. The women were Blake, Jones, and Mbutu. The men were Easley, Ramirez, Smith, Chin, and the tall blond one, Bueller. There were three other squads of Colonial Marines, thirty-two troopers in all, plus a skeleton ship's crew of nine. Counting herself, Wilks and the officer in charge, Stephens, that meant a total of forty-four people going to challenge an entire planet of the aliens.

There had been five times that many people on Rim, and only a single nest of the things there. And she and Wilks had been the only survivors. Not very encouraging.

She couldn't say how long she'd sat there blanked out, remembering, but Wilks pulled her back to the present. "I'm going to go shower," he said. "You going to be okay here?"

"Yes. I'm fine."

After Wilks left, Billie sat and stared at her cold food. The mess hall was not a large room. The other conversations were audible from time to time.

"Man, Stephens had a bug up his nose, hey?" Easley said.

"He's a groundpounder, what do you expect?" Chin said.

"Me, I think our sergeant is more than a little bit off the beam," Ramirez put in. "A few minutes short of an hour, if you know what I mean."

Blake pulled out a deck of cards. "Anybody for a little poker? Chin? Easley? Bueller?"

"Not me," Easley said. "I got walk-through duty. Keep a seat warm for me, though. Back in an hour." He stood and moved toward the door. There was a headset with throat pickup mike set into a recess there, and Easley took the com unit and slipped it on, nestling the earpiece into his left ear. "Watch Bueller, he deals from the bottom."

"Your ass, needledick," Bueller said.

"Big enough so your mother loves it," Easley said. He laughed and left.

Billie stared at her food. These guys did not know what they were up against, no matter what Wilks had told them. It was one thing to hear somebody tell it, another to face the things, to *feel* them.

Not something Billie wanted to do again, even though she knew she had to do it. Amazing how the memories came back. She felt as if she were a kid again. A scared kid.

Easley strolled down the corridor, the faux gravity making it feel almost like a walk through a building on Earth, maybe a bit lighter. He passed the first check station, flashed his lume into a couple of recesses the overheads didn't show, then spoke into the com, directly to the computer's recorder. "This is Easley, T. J., on walk-through duty, 1230 hours." He rattled off his serial number, the ship coordinates, and his findings: "Inspection so far reveals patent hull, no stress cracks, no animal or insect manifestations."

Yeah, and no runs, no hits, no errors.

This sucked, having to walk inspection. What did they make robots for? The things could see better, move faster, and they didn't care if they were missing a good poker game while they did it, either. This was make-work, Stephens was a by-the-tape commander, and next thing you knew he'd have them shining their boots and practicing close-order drill. Stupid.

Easley moved along, shining his light into dark

spots along the corridor, finding what he expected to find: nothing.

As he reached the aft quarter of his intended loop, he heard something. A faint, voicelike sound. He stopped. Sounded like it was coming from the number four cargo hold.

Easley hesitated. All walk-through was supposed to do was check the hull sandwich, not go poking into closed compartments. Whatever it was, it wasn't his business.

The sound came again. Almost like somebody talking very quietly.

Could be some kind of transfer echo, Easley thought. That happened sometimes. An air-conditioning vent picked up a voice on one part of the ship and transferred it somewhere else. The dense plastics and metals used on a no-frills military vessel did some strange things with vibrations. Easley remembered once being able to hear guys singing in the shower halfway around a T-2 troop ship.

Yeah, that's probably what it was. Besides, he was only supposed to do the hull, that was the drill, nothing else. He started to walk on.

There it was again.

Well, what the hell, he was curious. Might as well check it out, it wasn't like he had an appointment anywhere or anything.

He moved to the sliding door to the cargo area, thumbed the open pad.

"—*Benedict* to K-014, telemetry data uploading—"

Somebody was talking, no doubt about that, Easley heard. He moved through the cargo area, rounded one of the stack-boxes. Well, would you look at this. It wasn't an echo transfer, there the guy was, right in front of him. He had his back turned, Easley couldn't ID him.

"Hey," Easley began, "what are you—?"

That was as far as he got. The figure spun and then Easley felt a tremendous pain lance his throat, as if somebody had stabbed him there.

"Uhhh!" Easley sucked air, felt it impeded, reached for his neck. Felt his hands touch something wet and hot extending from his throat. As big around as his thumb, all the way through!

He tried to yell, found his voice wouldn't work. All he could manage was a wordless groan. The sound turned to a gurgle as warm liquid ran down his damaged windpipe. "Mmmm! Aaughh!"

He recognized the man who had done it, but he couldn't say the name.

Something slammed into his solar plexus, and what air Easley had was stolen. He . . . couldn't . . . breathe!

He bent forward, pulling at the spike through his neck. It started to move, despite the slippery fluid coating it.

Then something smashed his head and it all went gray.

On the *Benedict*'s bridge the tech monitoring ship's systems cursed. The pilot, busy feeding corrected stellar coordinates into his console, glanced over. "What?"

"I show the aft number two interior lock open."

The pilot glanced at his own board. "Yeah, I see it."

The tech said, "Is there a drill scheduled? Nobody told me."

"That's a negative. Nothing on the board. Call the lock and find out what the hell is going on."

"Copy." The tech spoke into his throat mike. "This is Systems Control. Who opened the inner door there?"

The tech waited. Nobody responded.

"I say again, this is Systems Control. Respond, whoever is in lock A-2."

Nothing.

"Where is the camera?" the pilot asked.

The tech's hands danced over the controls. "I'm not getting a signal from the monitor in the lock."

"Dammit! Call the jarhead commander and find out what's going on!"

"Colonel Stephens, this is Systems Control, do you read?"

The pilot looked at his own board. "Buddha. Where the hell is he?"

"Maybe he's taking a shower, got his unit off," the tech said. "Hello?"

"What?"

"The hatch is cycling closed."

"Well, that's something. Stupid marines ought not to be playing with the hardware—"

"Uh-oh."

The pilot looked at his board, saw the source of the tech's new worry. The outer hatch cycling open.

"I don't know what's going on, but I'm going to stop it right now," the pilot said. "We've got a corrective burn coming up and I sure as hell don't need a hole in the barn wall when it happens. I'm going to override and close that sucker."

"Affirmative that," the tech said.

The pilot worked a control.

"Uh-oh," the tech said.

Both their screens showed that the hatch cover was still open.

"Somebody is going to be in real deep shit," the pilot said.

"Got an EVA," the tech said. "Hull pickup is still working." The tech switched on the exterior lamps. "Look."

The image of a spacesuited figure tumbled slowly in their field of view, brightly lit by the outside floods.

"Who the hell is that? What is he doing out there?"

Easley awoke.

What?

His throat!

He reached for it, found the ribbing of the suit with the gauntlet. He was in vac, zero gee, in a suit. Fluid from his wound floated up and clouded the suit's visor. Frantically, Easley tried to speak. To call for help.

"Ungh! Gaugghh!"

He couldn't make words.

He twisted his head, trying to see where he was.

There, there was the ship, but it was moving away!

He reached for his tool belt, looking for a squirt can, to push himself back to safety.

The tool belt was empty.

Panic gripped him in cold fingers. He coughed, choking from the wound in his throat. He was going to die!

No, no, wait, wait! They'd spot him. You couldn't go EVA without the proximity detectors seeing you. The lights were on, they knew he was here. They'd send somebody out for him, it would only be a couple of minutes at the most. He'd be okay. They could patch him up—

Something drifted in front of his face. At first his obscured vision wouldn't let him see just what it was. He pulled his head back as far as it would go, blinked several times. A small cylinder, about the size of a roll of quarter-credit coins, floated up against the plate. He slowly turned and the ship's lights angled across his faceplate, giving him a better view. The cylinder had a digital counter on it—

The coldness stabbed Easley all the way to his bones.

The cylinder was an AP grenade. And the flashing numbers on it were going down.

Five . . . Four . . . Three . . .

"Nnnooo!" Finally, he managed a word.

It didn't help. He was going to—

The hull pickups polarized as the blast of light washed over them and the spacesuited figure shattered soundlessly into fragments. Body fluids crystallized almost instantly in the cold vacuum, spraying into frozen, colorless, gauzy clouds against pinpoints of distant stars in the blackness. Pieces of suit and flesh tumbled away, some hit the ship's armor harmlessly.

On the bridge, the tech said, "Oh, man."

The pilot merely nodded. What a way to die. He wondered if the guy knew what hit him. He hoped not.

15

In Houston, Likowski, James T., had been given the news.

There was a *thing* growing inside of him. Sooner or later, it was going to pop out of him like a birthday surprise, eating its way free, and when it was born, he would die. So long, Jim. Nice knowing you.

Simple.

He had been numb with the shock, and when that had worn off, the fear had claimed him. He was going to die.

Dr. Dryner and Dr. Reine were sorry, but there was nothing they could do.

"Can't you kill it? Cut it out?"

"Not without killing you," Dryner said. "It's a very tenacious life form." He was calm, as if he

were discussing the weather. Easy for him. He
didn't have a monster growing in his belly.

"Oh, God."

The two doctors stood next to where Jim sat on
the bed, both of them safely wrapped in cleansuits.
An armed guard stood just behind them, also
suited. He had a handgun holstered on his right
hip.

"So I'm like an incubation chamber for this
thing." It was not a question.

"Yes. Listen, if it is any consolation, your wife will
get the full insurance. She'll be taken care of."

"Oh, right, *that* makes me feel a whole lot better." The sarcasm made the words bitter. Now that
he knew what it was, he was sure he could feel the
thing moving inside him.

Getting ready to rip his guts out.

No!

"Hey!" he said, putting his hands over his belly.
He suddenly stood up next to the bed, made himself
sway a little.

The doctors showed concern.

"Likowski? Are you all right? James?"

"Telemetry, what's going on?"

They weren't worried about him, he realized, but
about their pet creature inside him. Damn them.

"I—something's happening!" He began to jerk,
as if losing muscular control. Yeah, something was
happening, all right, but not what they thought. He
snatched his arm away from Reine, slapping the
man's face in the process. He danced in a little half
circle, shivering.

Reine backed away. "Dammit!"

Come on, come on, get the guard over here!

"Give us a hand!" Reine ordered.

Good.

The guard, a burly man, wore his sidearm in a snatchproof rig, an old-style Delrin thumb-break strap keeping it safe in the holster. Jim knew about them, he'd done a tour in the Street Guard, they'd used the same kind of gear. If it had been a military hand ID unit, he wouldn't have a chance, but it wasn't, the guard was wearing gloves and the more sophisticated rig needed a bare hand for a print to register.

The guard grabbed him by the shoulders and Jim let himself be pushed toward the bed, where they could trigger the pressor field to hold him in place. "I'm—it's okay, it's gone now." He pretended to relax. "Thanks for the help," he said to the guard. He smiled.

When the guard smiled back from behind his clear faceplate, Jim reached down, rotated the thumb-break safety, popped the crow-tab, and pulled the gun from the holster. The weapon was a 4:4mm softslugger with a hundred-round magazine. The safety was in the trigger, it only had to be pulled. Jim twirled the pistol in his hand, pointed it at the guard, and fired.

Five rounds of hypervelocity softslugs tore into the man. The bullets were designed to mushroom on impact, to expend all of their energy on a human target without passing through the body. The entrance holes were small—the bullets would punch through class III body armor—but the missiles then expanded and dug craters the size of a baby's fist through vital organs.

The guard fell. He wasn't going to be getting up on his own.

Dryner and Reine turned to run, but Jim gave them two rounds each between the shoulder blades and they tumbled.

A siren hooted, over and over.

Jim turned to the mirrored wall and let go a dozen shots. The plastic chipped and shattered and he threw himself at it, falling through into a room with techs and more guards digging for weapons.

Jim came up, spraying the room. Men screamed and fell.

He paused long enough to dig out a spare magazine from the belt of a fallen guard, jamming it into the waistband of his hospital shorts. He ran.

Guards spilled into the hall. Jim shot them.

He found a keycard on a dead one next to the exit, waved the card at the scanner, and flattened himself against the wall as the door slid open.

Two guards came through, guns out. Jim emptied the last twenty shots in his softslugger into them. They fell like their legs had disappeared.

He ejected the empty magazine, snapped in the fresh one. Ran.

He made it to a building exit. Shot three unarmed people who tried to stop him. They didn't matter.

Outside it was hot, damp, the air had an oily stink, but that didn't matter, either. He was free.

He ran into the street. Behind him somebody yelled. He spun, fired a couple of shots, missed.

The softslugs spattered on the synstone walls like drops of dark paint dropped from a great height.

A hovercar fanned to a dragstop, almost hitting him.

Jim ran to the car, pointed the weapon at the woman driving. "Out!" he screamed.

The woman obeyed, terror in her eyes. He waved her away. She was a civilian, no reason to shoot her. He leapt into the car. Pulled the dragstop up, shoved the leaners on full. The car blew dust up, fanned away.

A round of hardball spanged against the car's body. A second tore through the canopy, but missed him by half a meter. Air whistled through the exit hole.

The car picked up speed. He had time to notice that the seats were vat-grown leather, a rich brown color, with the right smell. The control panel was real wood, burled and polished smooth.

They wouldn't catch him now.

At the complex's gate, a guard stepped out in front of the onrushing car, waving frantically for it to stop. She didn't have her gun out.

Jim ran the woman down. The car's front collision plate dented from the impact, the car slowed a little, but kept going. The gate was open.

The expressway entrance was ahead. It led through the city, to the suburbs. Where he and Mary had lived, before this happened. Where Mary was.

A police fanner rumbled into view behind him as he merged with the expressway traffic. The fanner flashed its lights. Vehicles moved aside to allow it room.

Jim put his car into full-speed mode. The whistling from the hole in the canopy went up in pitch, grew louder. The car was a hot machine, expensive, built for speed as well as looks, and quickly passed the speed limit.

The fanner was built to chase such cars, however. It gained on him.

The fanner would be armored. The softslugs wouldn't stop it.

They cranked up their hailer: "Stop your vehicle immediately! Houston Traffic Police!"

Jim laughed. What were they going to do? Give him a ticket? Take away his license?

The fanner pulled up level with him on his right. They were alone on the expressway now, the other traffic having dropped back or moved off to surface streets.

Jim looked at the two cops. In a second they would pull ahead of him and try to block him.

He had nothing to lose.

He shoved the control stick to the right. The car turned, slammed into the fanner. The traffic unit was larger, but he had inertia on his side. They veered toward the guardrail.

The fanner's driver tried to compensate, but too late. His engine screamed with power as he unleashed it, but the fanner dug into the rail, hit a support post, spun.

The impact slammed the fanner back into Jim's stolen car. Now both vehicles spun. Jim shoved his control forward, opened the drive fans to full again.

Slewed. Almost lost it and flipped, but powered out of the spin. Wobbled, then the gyros caught and held the car steady.

Not so lucky the cops. The fanner caught a rear blade on the rail, shattered the tough black plastic fan. Shards of jet sprayed. The loss of lift dropped the rear of the fanner. The friction flipped the vehicle like a man spins a coin on a table. The fanner smacked into the rail again, bounced, tumbled, and went over the side. It fell twenty meters and went through the roof of a fast-food shop.

Jim kept going.

He reached the resiplex where Mary was. Killed the fans. Got out, went to the building. Shot the guard who rose to stop him at the elevators.

The door to their unit opened. Mary's eyes went wide.

"Jim! I—they said—you were dead!"

"Not yet."

She reached out and they embraced. Hugged.

Down the hall, somebody yelled. "There he is!"

Of course. They would know where he lived.

"Good-bye, Mary. I just wanted to say that."

He twisted away from her, sprayed the hall. The slugs flattened on the walls as he waved the gun back and forth, ricocheted away, screaming almost like some tortured animal might.

"Aahh!" somebody said as they caught one.

"I have to go now, Mary. I love you."

It all felt unreal to him. Mary stood there, hands pressed to her face, as he turned and sprinted away.

He headed for the roof. Somebody would have a flier there he could steal.

Feet pounded behind him as he reached the roof. He found a flier with a card in the drive control. Smashed the door open. Got in. Lifted.

Bullets chewed at the flier, but he was off.

Where would he go? It didn't matter. He pointed the nose at the sun, shoved the power lever full on. Flew away. They'd never catch him. He was free. Free. Free.

But there was something large and ugly suddenly sitting in the seat next to him, something dark and monstrous. And his stomach started to hurt—

Likowski, James T. Lying on the pressor bed. His stomach hurt. Tears flowed from the outer corners of his eyes, ran down his face, pooled in his ears. The two doctors stood over him in their cleansuits, peering through protective faceplates, eyebrows raised. There was a guard behind them, but he wore no weapon. There was no need, and they would never have let anyone with a gun in here. Never.

All in his mind, Jim knew. A fantasy of escape that could not be.

The pain in his stomach increased, a sharp burning, as if a hot knife were being driven into him.

"Aahh!"

An amplified voice said, "Vital signs in flux, doctors! Heart rate up, blood pressure rising, myotonus pushing the limit."

Jim glanced at his own body. His bare flesh *bulged* suddenly, just under his sternum. The pain was incredible.

It was time!

Dryner reached out and touched the bulge on the patient's solar plexus. The skin immediately flattened. "Amazing," he said.

Reine said, "Get in here with the catch net!"

The man on the table screamed, a primal noise that set Reine's teeth on edge. Lord, what a sound! "Hurry up with that damned net!" Reine turned back toward the man on the table.

"Won't the pressor field hold it?" Dryner asked.

"I doubt it. Insufficient mass. Where the hell is the net?"

The amplified voice said, "Nobody is suited up out here, it'll take a minute—"

"This shouldn't be happening yet," Dryner said. "Our term estimates—"

"—were obviously wrong," Reine finished. "If somebody doesn't come through the lock in thirty seconds with that catch net I will fire the entire fucking staff!" he yelled. "None of you will ever work in this field again!"

To Dryner, Reine said, "This specimen is invaluable. Nothing can be allowed to happen to it, nothing!"

He leaned over the struggling man.

The patient screamed again. His flesh erupted, burst outward, and the alien's blind, toothed head came forth.

"Good God!" Dryner said, leaning away from it.

Reine, fascinated, leaned closer. "Why, look at it! Fascinating—"

"Here's the net!" somebody said.

Reine turned to look.

"Fuck!" Dryner said. "Look out!"

Reine twisted back toward the patient. Too slowly.

The thing shot out of the dying man. Impossibly fast, like a thick, armored, blood-slick arrow. It hit Reine's cleansuit, bit the osmotic material, and chewed through the heavy substance as if it were tissue paper.

Reine, horrified, stared at the thing.

"Bring the net!" Dryner yelled. "Hurry!"

Now Reine sought to bat at the thing, but its head was already inside the protective suit. He felt it reach his skin.

"Ahh! It's biting me! Get it off!"

Dryner reached for the thing's tail, but his gloved hands slipped on the gore that coated it. It moved away from his touch, pulling more of itself into Reine's suit.

"Help! Help me! Aahh! Oww!"

The tech with the catch net grabbed Reine, but the doctor twisted away from him in panic. In his fear, he tried to run from what was attacking him.

The inner hatch had not cycled closed. Reine ran for it.

"Louis, no! You'll breach isolation!"

Reine was beyond hearing, beyond caring. The only thing that mattered was that this *thing* was eating into him, burning like molten metal!

"Stop him!" Dryner yelled.

The tech reached for Reine, missed. Got in Dryner's way. They tangled, fell.

Dryner scrambled up, in time to see Reine clear the inner lock, lunge for the outer lock's control.

"Freeze the door controls!" Dryner yelled.

Too late. Reine pounded on the emergency override. The outer door slid wide. He staggered out into the hall.

Isolation was blown.

Dryner ran after his boss, yelling for him to stop.

"Kill it, kill it!" Reine screamed.

The security guards pulled their guns.

"No!" Dryner yelled. "Don't shoot it!"

The guard looked confused.

"Shoot him in the head!" Dryner commanded.

Now the guards really looked puzzled.

"Do it!"

The guards didn't move. Reine started to run. He might damage the specimen!

Dryner moved. He grabbed a gun from the nearest guard, who didn't try to stop him. Raised the weapon. Dryner had been a champion pistol shot while in college. Could have gone to the Olympics if he'd worked at it harder. He hadn't fired a gun in years, but the old reflexes were still there. Reine was only ten meters away. Dryner put the red dot square on the middle of the fleeing man's cleansuit helmet, took a deep breath, let part of it out, held it, and squeezed the trigger carefully, so as not to pull his aim off. At twelve meters now, it was an easy shot.

Reine's head shattered. He fell.

Dryner lowered the weapon. "Sorry, Louis," he said. "But you were the one who said how valuable the alien was. We can't chance hurting it."

The guards and techs stared at him.

"Now," he said, "bring the catch net."

He still had the gun. They all moved very fast.

And in the end, they didn't even need the net. Apparently the thing liked where it was. Good. That made it even easier.

16

Pindar the holotech lay on a table with a pressor field holding him down. He could turn his head, but that was about it. Since he was a tech, he knew how a pressor field worked, knew also it was impossible for an unaugmented man to break free of one. Even an expendable android built for short-term bursts of strength would have trouble with a functional pressor field, maybe it could escape, maybe not. That was an academic question, in any event. *He* wasn't going anywhere.

Two men in pearl-gray uniforms stood near the table, looking down at Pindar. The uniforms identified them as TIA, members of the Terran Intelligence Agency, and that was bad. Very bad. T-bags didn't stir themselves for menial crimes, only those that might threaten the security of the planet itself.

Pindar was in trouble, *aprieto mucho,* and he knew exactly why. Salvaje. After the last time with the man, Pindar had done some investigating on his own. He had stumbled across something he shouldn't know, something so terrifying he wanted to block it from his memory. And now, TIA had stumbled across him. He had known it was coming and he knew there was no way out.

One of the agents, a kindly looking man who could be somebody's grandfather, smiled at Pindar. He said, "Son, we have some questions we need answers to, if you don't mind."

The other agent, a lean, hatchet-faced young man with chocolate-colored skin, said, "You understand that we have full authority to question you in any manner in which we choose?"

Pindar licked dry lips. "*Sí.* Yes, I understand." Here it was. The beginning of the end. *Adios,* Pindar. Any way you look at it, you lose.

"Good," Grandfather said. He put a small plastic case upon the table next to the platform upon which Pindar lay. Opened the case. Removed from it a pressure syringe and a small vial of reddish fluid. Loaded the vial into the injector.

"I—I—there is no need for that," Pindar said. He hurried to get the words out. "I will answer your questions! I will tell you everything!"

Hatchet-face grinned, showing teeth that were too perfect to be natural. Vat-grown implants, had to be. "Oh, we know that, *Señor* Pindar. But this will save us all a lot of worry about how truthful your answers will be."

Grandfather leaned over Pindar, pressed the injector against the big artery in the tech's neck. Touched the firing stud. There was a small *pop!* and Pindar felt an icy rush begin in his throat, swelling to fill his head with coldness. *Dios!*

Hatchet-face looked at his chronometer. "Three. Four. Five. That's it."

Pindar felt the cold in his head change into a pleasant, muzzy warmth. It was okay. In fact, it was better than okay. He couldn't recall when he had felt so wonderful. His earlier worries evaporated like dew in the hot sunshine. Why, if he wanted to, he could get up off this table and leap into the air and fly like a bird! He didn't want to do that, though, he just wanted to lie here and visit with these nice men, Grandfather and Hatchet-face. After all, it was easy to see that they were his friends, and they cared deeply for him, and that anything he could do for them he should do, immediately.

"Feel good?" Grandfather asked.

"Yeah!"

"That's great. Mind if we ask you a few questions?"

"Why no, Grandfather, not at all!"

Orona leaned back in his chair. The TIA agent across from him wasn't wearing the pearl-gray uniform as regulations said he must while on duty, but there was no doubt about his identity. "Shall I run it?" he asked.

Orona nodded. "I hope you're wrong about this."

"They don't pay us to be wrong, Doctor. Sorry."

The agent touched a control on the holographic projector on Orona's desk. The air shimmered and the picture flowered. A close view of a man on a pressor table, smiling as if drugged.

"Tell us again," a voice off camera said. "Just like before."

"Sure," the man on the table said.

"After the last time, when Salvaje threatened me, I decided I had to find out more about what he was into.

"So I did some checking and discovered that he had hired other technicians to help him. I knew one of them slightly, Gerard, a contract worker for the Bionational Lab in Lima. I took the shuttle to Lima, made it a point to 'accidentally' bump into him. Bought him a few drinks. I learned that Salvaje had worked for Bionational before he started his crusade. Some kind of low-level administrator. He didn't need the money, he came from a rich family, but obviously he needed something from Bionat. Up and quit one day, but kept in touch with some of the techs. Gerard didn't know why Salvaje quit, and he only did some hardwiring for him, set up a small computer system. Salvaje paid well, that was all that was important.

"Gerard didn't know anything else about it, but that was enough. I knew that Salvaje had his own system.

"So I went to his place when he was visiting the pregnant whore and broke in."

The man on the table laughed. "His security was not so good as he thought. I got inside. Ran a download program and copied all his files. Took them home; he would never know I had been there.

"I found out where his messiah came from when

I ran an AV he had buried in a mathematical program."

The agent waved his hand and the image froze,
floating silently in the air. "You'll want to see this
while Pindar talks," he said. "We found it in his
computer."

The agent touched some controls. The man on
the table vanished and was replaced by a somewhat
grainy picture of Bionational's logo. The logo was
overstamped by a flaming red sign that said: Authorized Personnel, REQUIRED CLEARANCE TS-
1, Bionational Internal AV 42255-1, composite.

Pindar's voice continued.

"It was a bad induction copy of a Bionational top-
secret AV, for internal view only. Salvaje must have
stolen it or had somebody steal it for him. Whoever
had done it screwed it up, they lost part of the visual
and all of the audio track, so there's no sound."

The image blurred, then resolved into a view of a
clean room. A man lay on a table, bucking against
a field. A spot on his solar plexus tore open and
what appeared to be an eel's head the size of a
man's fist emerged, flashing bloody needle-sharp
teeth. Three men in cleansuits stood over the thing.
The eellike creature shot out of the man on the
table like a dart and latched on to one of the
cleansuited men. It ripped a hole in his suit.

"The first part of the recording showed the birth
of one of the things. Showed it attacking another
man."

The camera's view switched to another pickup,
zoomed in on the eel as it disappeared into the
cleansuit. The pickup pulled back to show the

terrified face of the man in the suit. He was screaming, but there was no sound. The image blurred, lost a couple of seconds, then re-formed.

Orona stared, fascinated.

The suited man ran. The camera lost him.

Two men fell as they tried to follow the fleeing one.

The image changed again. Armed guards stood in a corridor. A door opened and the cleansuited figure ran into view, slapping at a hole in his suit front. He lost control, shambled away.

The image jiggered. Another camera. The running man.

"They couldn't let it get away," the voice said.

The running man's head exploded, the cleansuit's helmet ballooned out, split, sprayed gore.

The image held, an angle on the body on the floor.

"Now," the agent said. "We switch to . . ."

A huge room. Armored walls. Looked like a containment vessel for controlled fusion experiments. Suspended from cables was a naked man's body. No doubt that he was dead; most of his head was gone.

A telemetry crawl ran across the image, but the figures and words were not those of a human.

"I didn't see it at first," came the voice. "But I figured it out fast enough when I saw the recording. They left the thing inside the guy they'd shot. He was a doctor, by the way, I saw that on the screen. Had been head of a division of Bionational before he became baby food.

"They put it in a place where it couldn't get out and they watched it."

The picture of the dead man froze.

"This is edited," the agent said. "Apparently this Salvaje couldn't get the other recordings, so this only hits the high points. Though he seems to have a hell of an organization, coded names and payouts, we're still working on those." He touched his control pad.

The image faded into another.

"Here's what it looks like about halfway grown," the agent said.

Orona stared. The thing appeared pretty much like the reconstruction on his own informational AV. But wait—*half* grown?

"Here is Salvaje's messiah," Pindar said. "It isn't a computer image as I thought, it is real."

The image faded again, went blank.

"Apparently neither Salvaje nor the technician were able to get past this point in the recording," the agent said. "But there is more. Our people have state-of-the-art recovery gear. We were able to pull another set of visuals from it."

The blank image faded in again.

This time the monster was larger, shaped slightly differently, with a massive cranial plate that branched antlerlike. It had an extra set of smaller arms coming from its chest area. The creature was huge, there was a scale built into the edge of the holo. The walls of the room were now covered with convoluted loops of shining black material, and the floor was dotted with garbage-can-sized eggs.

"My God," Orona said. "It's a queen!"

"One that doesn't need to be fertilized, apparently," the agent said.

Orona shook his head. "This could confirm my theory that a queen can develop from a drone as needed to continue the species. Some kind of hormonal change, perhaps."

The monster showed teeth, looking directly at the observation camera. The image faded and went blank again.

Orona waited.

"That's all there is of the stolen recording, I'm afraid," the agent said.

"Sweet baby Buddha's left nut," Orona said. "We've got to get it and those eggs. I'll make some calls, we'll seize the Lima laboratory in the interests of Terran Security."

The agent shook his head. "Too late for that."

Orona blinked. "What? What do you mean?"

"Watch."

The agent's hands did their magic with the control pad. The air lit with new pictures.

"These are from Bionational security monitors at the Lima complex. Note the date."

Orona looked at the red numbers in the corner of the image. Yesterday. Last night, from the hour.

"Apparently Salvaje had Pindar under a loose surveillance. Or perhaps an informant in the local police. Whatever. He must have found out we were closing in on him. Before Pindar's questioning had been completed, this is what happened at Bionational's Peruvian labs."

The scene was of a fenced perimeter. A guard kiosk. Two men sat inside.

"Hey, look at that!" one of them said.

Both guards jumped up. The road camera caught the approaching vehicle. An old-style windjammer thirty-ton cargo truck approaching the gate. At speed.

"Stop, you asshole!" one of the guards yelled.

The truck slammed into the gate. The gate was durasteel mesh and solid wrist-thick bars and had not been designed to withstand the impact of a multiton cargo truck moving at fifty kph. The metal bent, bolts tore loose, wire stretched . . . but even so, it held. The truck slewed to a halt against it.

From the ruined cab of the vehicle, a single battered woman crawled out, managed to stand. She wore a robe. The security computer locked a wide-angle camera onto her. Her face was bloody. Her hands were empty but she had something strapped to her chest, a blocky circular device about the diameter of a dinner plate.

One of the guards hit the panic button and the alarm Klaxon started hooting. The other guard pulled his sidearm and ordered the woman to halt.

She kept coming. As the guard raised his weapon to fire, the woman exploded. The image washed white.

"Buddha," Orona said.

"We IDed the bomb as a five-ton building demolition charge," the agent said. "It took out the kiosk, the truck, and twenty-six meters of fence."

A patrol robot provided the next segment of recording.

The POV shot as the robot approached the destroyed entrance to the compound was a little shaky, despite the minicam gyros in the bot, because of the rubble it was traversing, the agent said.

Orona watched, fascinated.

The bot broadcast its security warning as a stolen passenger bus stuffed full of people roared past it. Since a security alert had been called the bot's guns were armed and it was authorized to fire upon intruders. It sprayed the bus with twin 10mm machine guns; its cameras picked up the holes as the rounds pierced the heavy plastic sides of the bus. People were dying inside, that was apparent, and the bot continued firing, aiming for the operator. A warning light began flashing on the bot's proximity detectors, and the bot reacted to the new target, shifting on its axis, just in time to be smashed by a speeding aircar. The driver, who died in the subsequent explosion as he and the car and the bot were engulfed in a yellow flash, died smiling.

"This next piece we got from a spysat we had footprinting the area," the agent said.

The view was from overhead, and had that too slick look that an augmentation computer added to a pixilated image. Three buses approached the large building centered in the frame. Security robots fired on the vehicles, and return fire came from the buses at the defensive bots.

The first bus reached the complex's entrance. Ten or twelve robed figures scrambled out and ran for the door. From the angle, Orona couldn't tell if they were men or women, but it didn't matter, because they were cut down by gunfire from within the building.

Another dozen figures boiled forth from the bus.

Yet more from the next bus that arrived, and a fourth wave from the final bus. Nearly all of them were slaughtered, too.

Nearly all of them.

One of the figures tottered to the door.

The spysat's filters cut down the white blast as the figure blew apart. Smoke and debris sprayed from the building.

"Got the door and the guards there," the agent said. He spoke as if he were talking about what he had for lunch.

More figures emerged from the buses.

The images wavered.

"Spysat moved out of range there," the agent said. "We didn't have anything else we could shift over for another few minutes. This piece is from the building's security comp. Watch."

A lone guard, one of his legs missing, lay on the floor, a suppressed machine gun in his hands. He fired the weapon, waving it back and forth.

The wounded guard's targets were robed figures, men and women, smiling as they walked into the hard sleet of bullets. Ten, fifteen, maybe a score of them fell before the guard's gun ran dry.

The camera caught perfectly the woman who bent over the wounded guard and put a thin knife blade through his eye. She was smiling as if this were the funniest thing she had ever seen.

More figures moved into view.

"Freeze frame," the agent said.

The moving figures turned into an oil painting, clear, sharp, still. "Nice optics," the agent said. He pointed at the hologram. "See that one, second from the right?"

Orona nodded.

"Salvaje."

Orona regarded the bearded man. He didn't look like a fanatic. But then—what exactly *did* a fanatic look like? Was he supposed to be drooling and foaming at the mouth?

"Resume play."

More robed people arrived. Orona estimated there must be at least thirty-five or forty of them who had survived the attack.

"Thirty-seven passed this camera," the agent said, as if reading Orona's thoughts.

The image cut to a view of a door. DANGER, it said in ten-centimeter-high letters, BIOLOGICAL EXPERIMENT. Authorized Personnel Only.

A pair of dead guards lay on the floor. One of them had a thin knife stuck in his eye. Five robed figures sprawled near the guards.

"Thirty-two of them left," the agent said.

Another angle. Inside the chamber. Orona recognized the ropy exudate on the walls. A translucent mist fogged the ground, partially covering rows of eggs.

Some of the attackers stripped off their robes, showing themselves naked underneath. They each had a tattoo of a drone alien on their bodies, extending from neck to pubis.

"God*damn*," Orona said.

"We found the tattooist, he was one of them. Been making house calls for months, apparently. It gets better," the agent said. "Check this part."

The queen alien lumbered into view. She stared at the people, twisted her head to one side, then the other, as if puzzled.

Salvaje faced her. He said something, but only a few words were audible.

"—be one with you, Messiah!"

"Sorry about the sound," the agent said. "We're lucky we got this much. We found the blue box almost six klicks away."

Orona looked at the agent. "What?"

"I'll explain. Watch."

Some of the eggs began opening. Half of the invading people now stood naked, arms outstretched, eyes closed, waiting. The others remained well outside the room, one angle showed them. "We've cut together several views here," the agent said.

The first one to open was in front of Salvaje. He stood with his arms wide, as did the others, but his eyes were open. He leaned down over the egg. The flaps glistened with strands of shining slime. Fingerbonelike legs emerged and caught the edges of the opened egg, hauling the primary-embryo stage of the alien's crablike body onto the lip. It leapt at Salvaje, wrapped a muscular tail around his neck, jammed its ovipositor into his startled mouth, and clutched his face with the legs, pressing itself flat against his face.

Orona could see the terror grip the man, and he realized that in this final moment of truth, the reality was more than he had bargained for, for Salvaje tried to scream.

The sound was choked off by the tube rammed down his throat.

The scientist in Orona was intrigued, but the human part of him recoiled.

Other eggs splayed wide their fleshy openings, other primary-embryos leapt upon waiting faces.

The queen watched it all impassively.

Then, when all of the naked humans had been infected, the outermost eggs hatched and depleted of their inhabitants, the remaining robed people darted in and dragged their comrades away, adroitly avoiding, save for one, being attacked by the remaining eggs.

The queen did not approve of this, but she was anchored to her huge egg sac and could not move quickly enough to catch the scurrying humans.

"Normally there would be drones to hold them," Orona said.

"What?"

"Never mind."

The door shut. The queen raged.

As the attackers hauled away their fellows, one of them spotted the watching camera. He pulled a handgun and fired at it. He missed three times, but the fourth shot wiped the screen.

"What happened?"

The agent shrugged. "The security system was overridden at this time. We have no more images of the fanatics."

"Overridden?"

"One of Bionational's chief security people sent a coded squirt to the system. Self-destruct code."

"What?"

"Ninety seconds later the security system destroyed itself—along with the entire complex. Blew it to bits."

"No! What about the alien? The eggs?"

"Scattered about the countryside in pieces the size of your little fingernail, Doctor."

"Oh, no!"

Orona was stunned by the news. What a waste! He'd sent a ship halfway across the galaxy to obtain such specimens and if they'd been a few hours quicker, they could have had one right here on Earth! *That* explained the dreams people had been having! Damn! Damn!

Wait. Ninety seconds. Could that mean—?

"What about the fanatics? Did any of them get away? There were at least a dozen of them infected!"

The agent sighed. "We don't know. Our people have been combing the country looking for them, but there's no sign of them. The explosion was in the half-megaton range. There's no way to tell from the wreckage how many people died in it, whether anybody got away."

For a moment hope flared in Orona. There might be a chance.

"We hope none of them did," the agent said.

"What? Are you crazy? These life forms are priceless!"

"Think about it, Doctor."

Orona was a brilliant man; he had always been at the top of any class he was in. It hit him, what the agent was trying to say. Yes, the aliens were priceless. But under controlled circumstances. Bionational knew that. That's why the complex was rigged to blow up if there came a breach in security. If the alien somehow escaped, got free of captivity, that could be disastrous. Even a single egg was potentially dangerous. Given how quickly they could breed and come to maturity, given how they could change into queens if the need was there . . .

Orona nodded. Yes. He saw it.

A dozen queen aliens, hiding out, laying eggs, that could be a problem.

That could be a major problem.

17

Billie stood in front of one of the "viewing ports," watching the streams of light strung like thin, crooked tubes of bright neon across the dark background. She hadn't spent much time in space, not since she had been a child, and this kind of travel was new to her. She stared, trying to remember her parents during happy times, but their bloody end kept jamming itself into her thoughts. Since Wilks had come to see her that first time, the reality the doctors had tried to wipe kept bobbing to the surface like floats on a pond. The truth was rising and would not be denied. All the dreams that had been real . . .

"That's an illusion, you know," came a voice from behind her.

Billie turned and saw one of the marines, Bueller, standing there.

"The improved gravity drive means we can spend less time in hypersleep, but the multidimensional matrices of the butterfly field turn dots into lines. Something to do with some esoteric particle, chronons, or impiotic zuons or some such."

"I wonder what Easley saw in his last seconds?" she said.

It was a rhetorical question, but Bueller shook his head. "I don't know. I can't imagine why he would have gone EVA and taken a grenade with him."

"Some kind of depression, the colonel says. Maybe Easley was running from monsters."

Again Bueller shook his head. "I don't think so. We were pretty close. It doesn't make any sense that he would suicide. Besides, there are a lot easier ways."

Billie nodded. Blowing yourself to bits in deep space was not her choice of an entry to the final chill.

"I don't trust Stephens," Bueller said. "He doesn't have any command experience in the field and I think he wanted to hush the whole thing up. If we're successful in our mission—whatever it *is* exactly—then up-levels will overlook a few bodies. But if we fail, then the little things will count."

"I hate to disillusion you, Bueller, but if this mission doesn't succeed, we'll get eaten by things with big teeth, or else turned into puppy chow for the baby things with little teeth. We'll all end up on the cold ground as lumps of alien dung for the bugs to fight over."

"How colorful," Bueller said.

"Telling it like it is. I've seen these things work."

"You sound like Wilks." He stood there for a second and she could see he was uncomfortable.

"Come on," Billie said. "I'll buy you a cup of what passes for coffee."

"Okay. Yeah."

In the mess hall, Ramirez was waiting for a self-heating meal packet to cook. He grinned at Billie and Bueller when they came in.

The two of them sat at an expanded plastic table with their paper cups of the vile ship's brew.

"Wilks must really think a lot of you to bring you along. You know Stephens will hang him out to twist when we get back, no matter what face-saving shit he's telling us now."

Billie sipped the coffee, made a face. "Yeah. Wilks and I, we understand each other."

"I'll bet," Ramirez said as he put his tray down on the next table. "Wilks, he's an expert on cradle-robbing, hey?"

"Shut up, Ramirez," Bueller said.

"Hey, man, I'm all for a little pussy myself, but not so green—"

Bueller came up, caught Ramirez under the chin with the V of his thumb and fingers, and shoved him back against the wall. "I said shut the fuck up!"

Ramirez's voice was choked when he tried to speak. "Hey, man, fuck, let go!"

Billie saw the tendons in Bueller's hand standing out. He was practically holding the bigger man off the floor, pinned to the wall like a struggling insect. He seemed too strong for a man his size.

Abruptly Bueller relaxed, pulled his hand away.

Ramirez rubbed at his throat. "You're crazy, man, you know that?" He turned and walked out of the room, leaving his steaming dinner behind.

"Why did you do that?" Billie asked.

Bueller looked flustered, embarrassed. "He's got a big mouth and he shoots it off too much."

"That's it?"

"Yeah."

Billie let it alone. There was something else here, but she wasn't sure what it was. She wasn't sure she wanted to know what it was.

In his quarters on the chase ship, Massey sat *seiza* and concentrated on his breathing. He had never learned to meditate as the masters did, but he could use it to calm his system. Sure, he exercised his body, practiced fighting techniques, drilled over and over again with weaponry, but these things brought him no joy. They were to keep him crisp, to maintain his cutting edge, nothing more. Being in top shape was part of the business, necessary, and he trained himself as if he were a prized show animal, proper diet, enough rest, technical mastery as required, no more, no less. He was the equal of any serious athlete, and against the few who might be in better physical shape or with faster reflexes, he augmented himself with drugs or figured ways to cheat. If you wanted a man dead, it was better to shoot him in the back from long range than to stand facing him like some holovid hero. That was a fool's game, and since the last man standing was the victor, it was always better to slant things your way when possible.

Soon another test would come. He must be ready for it. So he sat, but it was not mindless meditation but mindful scheming that filled him. In a contest like this, there could be no second-place winner. To be second was to be last and to be last here was to be dead.

"Have you got a first name?" Billie asked as they toured the magazine. Here were racks of carbines, canisters of gas, grenades and other hardware, all securely stored under the QM's seal.

Bueller said, "Yes. Mitchell."

"Mitchell," she said, testing the word. "Mitch?"

"If you like."

Billie turned to look at the racks of small arms under their kleersteel cases. Bueller put a hand on her shoulder, to point her toward the display model.

"Don't touch me," she said.

He snatched his hand away. "Oh. Sorry. I didn't mean anything by it."

"It's okay. In the hospital, when somebody put their hands on you it almost always meant you were in trouble. After the hand came a derm-patch or an injector, to fill you with chem that made you sluggish and stupid."

He sighed. "Yeah, I can understand that."

"Can you? Do you know what it's like living most of your life in a medical unit full of crazy people?"

"No," he admitted. "But I've spent my share of time in hospitals. Not fun places."

He changed the subject. "Here, here's the basic weapon we're using on this mission." He pulled the demo model, a dummy, from the rack. "This here is your four-point-eight-kilo-fully-automatic-electronic-blowback-operated-caseless-ten-millimeter-M41-E carbine," he said, as if reciting a litany. "It has an effective range of five hundred meters, holds either a one-hundred-round magazine of antipersonnel, a one-hundred-round magazine of armor-piercing, or a seventy-five-round magazine of rainbow tracer ammunition, and mounts a thirty-millimeter pump-operated grenade launcher under the barrel with a range of one hundred meters. Officially."

He grinned. "Unofficially, you can't hit anything smaller than a subway car past a couple hundred meters 'cause the sights are for shit, and if the grenade goes farther than fifty meters before it hits the ground, you must have a god who likes you.

"At close range, however, this is a mean machine and you don't want to be on the receiving end in anything less than full class-VII spidersilk armor or you get turned into bloody mush."

He held the weapon out. "Take a look. It won't bite."

Billie held her smile in check. The model number had changed, but the basic weapon was not that different from the one she had dreamed about. No, not dreamed about, *remembered*. This part of the dreams had come back to her dozens of times over the years, the instructions that Wilks had given her were burned into her as if branded by white-hot metal.

She took the carbine, thumbed the magazine catch, and popped the dummy, checked to be sure it was empty, then slammed the magazine back into place. She cycled the action twice to make certain the chamber was cleared, then stroked the grenade launcher's pump twice to make sure the loading tube was empty. She pulled the weapon to her shoulder, sighted at the far wall, both eyes open, and dry fired the piece. The electronic trigger was rigged to make an audible click for such practice and did so. She lowered the weapon, twisted it to present arms, and tossed it at Bueller. It had been more than a dozen years, she had not touched such weapons in all that time, but it was like she knew it would be. Except that the weapon felt so much smaller and lighter now than it had when she was ten.

He was surprised, but managed to catch the carbine without dropping it.

"Trigger's a little stiff and it's got some creep," she said. "Your armorer should run a diagnostic on it when he gets the chance." She was showing off, but what the hell.

He laughed. "I'm impressed. Where'd you learn to do that?"

"I ran with a rough crowd when I was a kid." She paused, then said simply, "The things we're going to go hunt, they killed my family and everybody I knew."

"Buddha," he said. "I'm sorry."

She shrugged. "What about you? You have family?"

"No. The marines are my family."

Billie thought about that for a second. Well. Other than going off to get killed they had something else in common. No family.

"Listen, about Sergeant Wilks," he began. "If you've got something going with him—"

She cut him off. "When the aliens took over our colony, Wilks and his squad came down. He and I were the only ones left who got off-planet before they sterilized it. He saved me. I was ten years old. That was the last I saw of him until a few days before we left Earth."

"I'm sorry, I don't mean to pry—"

"Sure you do. That's okay. I've been pried open by experts. I got used to it."

He stared at his feet.

"Let me ask *you* something," she said.

"Okay. That's fair."

"Why'd you really grab Ramirez in the mess hall?"

He sighed. "What he said about you and Wilks. I didn't want it to be true."

"Why not?"

He shook his head, stared at his feet again.

It hit her why all of a moment. Buddha and Jesus in a hammock, Billie, you been taking stupid pills again? This guy *likes* you! Not like one of the orderlies who felt you all over when tucking you in bed, or who took out their dongs and jacked off on you when you were lying there so stoned you couldn't move, he's *concerned* about you!

We're going off to get killed and here's this marine falling for you. How about that.

Suddenly she saw him in a new light. He was her age, he had nobody but the marines and they were sending him off to die. He was lonely. She knew what that felt like.

She reached out, touched him on the shoulder. "Hey," she said. "Mitch."

He looked up from his boots, his gaze bright, pale eyes clear and searching. "Yeah?"

"Why don't you show me some more of the ship?"

He grinned, like a kid with a new toy. "Yeah. I'd like that."

Billie was fairly certain she was going to like it, too.

18

The agent said to Orona, "No. Nothing new on possible survivors of the explosion in Lima. There are some rumors floating around about a cult talking over a ranch in New Chile; we're checking it out. Other than that, nothing." He shrugged.

Orona merely nodded. In this case, no news was bad news.

Massey checked his timers for the fifteenth time. Soon. Very soon. The last squirt update said they were within a light-year of their destination. Practically there, as fast as the new gravity drives could move the ships. Getting close. Getting ready.

Wilks had given Billie a couple of make-work chores, checking systems, cargo manifests, like that. When he arrived at the midship comp terminal kiosk, he expected to see her there.

He didn't expect to see somebody with her. Somebody like Bueller, with his hand possessively on the girl's shoulder, kneading the muscle gently.

"Bueller," Wilks said. "You have business in here?"

The marine jerked his hand away from Billie's shoulder.

Billie turned. "Wilks. Mitch was only—"

He cut her off. "Yeah, I can see what *Mitch* was 'only' doing. Take a hike, Bueller."

"Dammit, Wilks!" Billie said. "Who the hell do you think you are?"

"Me? I'm the guy who pulled you out of the chemical fog you were living in, just before they were ready to strain your brain and throw your mind out."

Billie flushed, stared at him. She owed him, he knew that, and he knew she was holding her comment because of it.

"I thought I told you to take a hike."

Bueller smoldered. He was on the edge of swinging at him; Wilks could feel the rage like heat from a furnace. He hoped Bueller's sense of duty was stronger than his anger: if he let go, Wilks wouldn't be able to take him—Bueller was younger, faster, stronger, better-trained. He would have to shoot him and Wilks wasn't sure that would stop him in time, given the tightness of the quarters.

But Bueller stalked out, not saying anything.

Billie rounded on him. "All right, Wilks, I owe

you, but that doesn't give you the right to tell me
who I can talk to!"

"I saw you," Wilks said. "You were doing more
than talking."

Billie's eyes went wide. "Are you jealous? Damn,
Wilks!"

"Not jealous, kid. Just trying to save you grief."

"I'll handle my own grief, thank you! I'm not a
child and you aren't my father!" With that, she
turned and marched out.

Wilks stared at her as she left. He shook his head.
Maybe he was too burned out. Maybe she just liked
having somebody pay attention to her. Maybe he
should tell her the rest of it.

No. Maybe none of them were going to ever get
home; even if Billie did, the whitecoats would be
waiting for her. Maybe she should enjoy whatever
free time she had left.

Lotta maybes there.

So, no. He wouldn't tell her. He'd tried to warn
her, that was the best he could do. Like she said,
she'd have to handle her own grief.

One way or another, grief was coming, that was
for damn sure.

They'd dragged a cushion into the forward storage compartment, between two rows of hex cartons
that effectively formed corridors in the room. It was
dim, quiet, and nobody was going to happen across
them accidentally. There was a door alarm rigged
to chime if anybody even stuck their head into the
room.

They sat facing each other on the cushion, and

Billie rubbed her hand against the hard muscle in Mitch's arm, feeling the smoothness of it. His strength appealed to her, it made her feel safe.

"I'm sorry about Wilks," she said. "He was out of line."

"Maybe not," Mitch said. "Maybe I don't know what I'm doing here."

"I know," Billie said. She reached up with both hands and caught his face. It was smooth, his beard depilated so close that his skin felt softer than her own. She urged him to her, kissed him. Slipped her tongue into his mouth.

The heat of his passion flared, and he circled his arms around her; she could feel the power of him even though he held her loosely. The kiss grew more intense. Billie felt her heart speed up, her breathing turn ragged.

He slipped one hand under her shirt, cupped her breast.

Oh, yes!

Eagerly she tugged his coverall tabs open, the *critch* of the cro separating loud in the quiet room. Felt his hairless chest, the thick muscles bunched under her touch. Slid her hand down, and found a different kind of hardness.

He moaned, a soft, wordless sound of desire.

He slid his mouth down her neck, pulled wide the tabs on her shirt and pants, moved farther down, kissing his way over her breasts and belly and beyond.

"Oh, yes!" she said. She could hardly breathe.

After another moment she didn't worry about breathing anymore.

* * *

Afterward, Billie and Mitch lay in a tangle of arms and legs. She was sweaty and her pulse had slowed some, but she wasn't tired. Just . . . fulfilled.

There had been others. Even in a hospital they couldn't watch you all the time, and Billie had been with a male patient once, and another time an orderly. And there had been a couple of women, too. But nothing like this. It had never felt so good, seemed so right, been so joyous as this linking with Mitch.

Mitch said, "I've never done this before."

She smiled. "Really? Could have fooled me. You were terrific."

"Was I?"

"Well, not that I have all that many guys to compare you to myself, but, yeah, you were."

He laughed softly. "Good. I wanted to be, for you. I—well, I love you, Billie."

Billie drank it in, the feeling, the touching, what he said. Yes. She'd been waiting her whole life for this, had never expected it to happen, never really believed such a thing was possible for somebody like her. But here it was.

"I'm glad. I love you, too, Mitch."

He shifted slightly and she felt his renewed interest poking at her. "My, my. Potent, aren't we?"

He bit at his lip. "There's something I need to tell you," he said.

"Showing is better than telling," she said. "Why don't you show me how this works instead?" She touched him lightly with one hand. "We can talk later."

"Okay. I take your point."

"No, sweetie, I'll take *yours.* . . ."

Jones was taking her turn at the proximity sensor board. Ten minutes into her tour, a bogie began blipping at her.

"Well, shit," Jones said. She wasn't deep in this kind of work but since the computer did most of it, all she had to do was ask. "What do we have here, folks?"

The computer ran a crawl across the hologram.

Jones shook her head. "Can't be, pal. There ain't supposed to be another ship out here."

"Problem?" came a voice from behind her.

Colonel Stephens stood there.

Jones said. "Sir, the PS says there's a vessel out there only a hundred klicks back and closing. The thing musta blown a circuit or something, right?"

"Could be an echo, that happens," Stephens said. "Run a diagnostic."

"Affirmative, sir." Jones touched a button.

The image gridded, words sprayed across it, and the result came up almost immediately: DIAGNOSTIC CHECK COMPLETE, ALL SYSTEMS FUNCTIONAL.

"Damn," Jones said. "Excuse me, sir. There *is* a ship out there. I'll sound General Alert." She reached for the red button cover, started to flip it up so she could reach the alarm control.

"No," Stephens said.

"Sir, if that's a ship we have to assume it's hostile to our mission, that's SOP—"

By now, Jones had turned enough to see that

Stephens had drawn his side arm. An issue softslug pistol.

"Sir!"

He shot her. Through the left eye. Gore spattered on his coverall as Jones's head snapped back and smashed into the sensor board. She slid from the chair, dead before she reached the deck.

"Sorry," Stephens said, reholstering his weapon.

The colonel waved his hands over the com unit. "Stephens here," he said. "We are go for mating."

"Copy that," came Massey's voice from the com. "We are on the way."

Wilks was in the rec room working out on the myoflex full range-of-motion gear when the ship shook. He didn't know what, but something had hit them. Damn! Anything smaller than an asteroid should have been deflected by the shields!

Wilks jumped from the machine and grabbed his clothes.

There was a General Alert button near the door. Wilks broke the cover and slapped it with one hand, hardly slowing as he ran.

Billie was putting her shirt back on over tender breasts when the vibration rocked her hard enough to knock her from her feet. She hit one of the hex cartons and bounced off, managed to land on her butt without doing any damage.

Mitch absorbed the rocking with his legs and stayed up.

A klaxon began screaming, *reeh-aww, reeh-aww*, over and over.

"That's General Alert," Mitch said, tabbing his coverall shut.

"It's a drill, right?" Billie said, getting up.

"Maybe," he said, "but I don't think so. Something hit us."

"Maybe it was an engine going out?"

"No, we'd all be atomic dust, that happened. I can't believe they'd run a drill this close to the destination. Something is wrong."

He started for the exit, then stopped. "Listen, Billie, stay here, okay? Until I see what it is."

"Wait a minute—"

"Please? This is a pressurized area, if there are leaks anywhere, you'll be okay here. Please. I'll be back as soon as I can."

Billie nodded. "Okay. Listen, Mitch, be careful!"

"I will. I love you."

"I love you, too."

He grinned, then turned and sprinted away.

Ramirez came out of the shower wrapped in a towel as Bueller ran past. "What the fuck is going on?"

"Got me," Bueller said. "We've got to get to the armory and load up; our stations are next to the APC; we're supposed to be locked and loaded in a GA."

"I know, I know." Ramirez grabbed a coverall hanging on the door and tried to run and put it on at the same time. He didn't manage either very well.

"Jones is on watch, right?" Bueller said, glancing at his chronometer.

"Got me, man."

Mbutu stepped into the corridor ahead of them and started toward the armory.

"You seen Wilks?" Bueller yelled at her.

"Nah, ain't seen nobody, I was sleepin'," she hollered back at him.

They reached the armory. Chin had armorer duty and had already lifted the kleersteel covers. He started handing out weapons. Half of 2nd Squad was there, most of 3rd. Bueller didn't see any of 4th or anybody else from his own, 1st.

"Shit!" somebody from 3rd Squad said.

"What?"

"This piece is missing the feed ramp, asshole!"

Chin looked at the carbine he was about to hand to another trooper. "Sah! So is this one! Weapons check, marines!"

It only took a few seconds.

All of the carbines were missing the feed ramps.

Electronic feed ramps were critical. Without them, the only way anybody was going to do any damage with one of these pieces would be to whack somebody over the head with it.

"Oh, shit," Chin said. "We got a big problem."

"What about the grenades?" somebody asked.

"Buy a brain, stupid," Chin said, "you want to set off a fucking grenade on a *starship*?"

Somebody else waved a handgun. "These are rascaled, too. Somebody don't want us to be shootin' nothin'."

Bueller said, "You got hands and feet, marines, you been trained to use them. Get moving."

The intercom came to life. "This is Colonel

Stephens. All marines report to the aft loading bay immediately. Repeat, I want all marines to report to the aft loading bay immediately."

Wilks still had his unregistered civilian stunner, and he had it in hand when he heard boots clattering through the lock. Company coming, and not anybody he was expecting. He lit the target laser. The first few through the hatch were his. He took a deep breath, lined the laser's dot up on the hatch at eye level, and waited.

"Put your weapon down," came a voice from behind him. "Try to turn around and you're dead."

Stephens!

Wilks said, "Sir, we're being boarded!"

"I know all about it. Drop the stunner."

Whatever this was all about, Stephens had him cold. He'd never get around in time. Wilks dropped the weapon.

The hatch slid up and assault-suited men sprinted through the opening, splitting into two groups, one heading fore, the other aft. Two of them brought their hardware to bear on Wilks: these were automatic shotguns that fired frangible epoxy-boron-lead pellets. They didn't have much penetration, but against an unarmored human target, they were deadly enough. They didn't call them splatter-guns for nothing. Wilks raised his hands.

The last man sauntered into the ship proper, an antique 10mm recoilless Smith DA-only pistol in one hand. He waved the gun at Wilks. "Hello, marine. New in town?"

"Right on schedule, Massey," Stephens said.

"Of course. I've got him. You can put your piece away."

Wilks felt his guts twist. Stephens was a traitor. He didn't know who this Massey was or who he represented—one of the war cartels, maybe, some corporation—but Stephens had sold them out.

Wilks turned. "You killed Easley, didn't you?"

Stephens was holstering his sidearm. "It was necessary."

"Bastard."

"Life is hard, Wilks. A man has to do things to get by."

The one called Massey grinned. "Glad to hear you say that, Colonel." He pointed his gun at Stephens. "Move to the side there, would you, Sergeant?"

Stephens blinked, his mouth gaping in shock. "Wh-what are you doing?"

"A man who would sell out his command can hardly be trusted, wouldn't you agree?"

"W-w-wait a second! We had a deal! You *need* me!"

"The deal is off. And I don't need you anymore."

He fired the pistol.

The gun made a loud *whump!* in the corridor. Wilks's ears rang with the noise.

Stephens grew a crater in his chest. As he fell, the crater turned bright red. Arterial blood from the shattered heart, Wilks knew. Dead meat.

Wilks looked at Massey.

"No, don't worry, Sergeant, I'm not going to kill you, unless you do something foolish. You and your marines will be useful. You know anything about, ah, fishing?"

Wilks stared at him as if he had turned into a giant lizard.

Massey laughed. "If you want to catch a fish, you have to have the right kind of bait."

Massey laughed louder, as if at a private joke, but Wilks understood exactly what the man meant.

Because Wilks knew exactly what the aliens ate.

19

After waiting for an hour, Billie crept to the comp panel inset next to the storeroom's door and carefully switched it on. She managed to activate a monitor after a little effort, and what she saw was three marines being herded down a hall by two strange men with guns.

Billie sucked in a fast breath. What was going on?

A few minutes with the computer gave her very little more. The ship was in the hands of some invading group. Who were they? Why had they attacked the ship? How had they managed to overcome a military vessel full of armed marines?

What about Wilks and Mitch?

She couldn't find Mitch, but some switching did give her an image of Wilks. He was being held at gunpoint by a tall, fair-haired man.

Oh, gods! What was she going to do?

The man talking to Massey was strange, Wilks saw, and after a moment he realized why—the man was an android, one they hadn't bothered to do a full cosmetic on. Must be an expendable. And, Wilks also realized, one that didn't worry fuck-all about the First Law for robots and androids, never to kill a human. How in the hell had the pirate managed to pull that one off?

"Is everybody accounted for?" Massey asked.

"Yes, sir," the android replied. "We lost two units during the operation. Four marines died as a result of wounds incurred during takeover; two more are seriously injured. Two marines were killed by Stephens previously. We have all the remaining marines and ship's crew in custody, cross-checked and matched, although there is an anomaly."

"What's the problem?"

"The initial marine head count after hypersleep arousal shows plus one."

Massey turned to look at Wilks. "Well?"

"Stephens miscounted. He was a stupid asshole."

Massey said to the android, "Double-check the names and ID numbers. We don't need any loose cannons onboard."

"Sir."

"You got balls, whoever you are," Wilks said. "To attack a government ship. What's the point?"

"To keep a greedy competitor from stealing my company's money."

"Competitor? If you represent a company you

should know the government doesn't compete with private concerns."

"Sure it does. They want to round up some of these valuable aliens and develop them as weaponry. You don't think they'll sell the results to anybody with the money to pay for them?"

Wilks shook his head. "You don't know what you're fucking with here. These things have wiped out a couple of colonies."

"I know more than you think, Sergeant. You see, we already *have* one of these things. On Earth. Our mission here is to make sure nobody else gets one before we can exploit our advantage. That, and gathering whatever information we can to help things along. Their favorite food, lighting, environment, like that. For all we know, these things aren't the top dogs on their world. They could be like mice."

"You have an alien? On Earth?"

"Yep. I haven't seen it myself, but I understand it's an ugly beast."

"Buddha!"

"He can't help you, Sergeant. I'm your god now."

Billie huddled against a crate, thinking. She could probably hide here for a long time without anybody finding her. She wasn't listed on the crew or marine manifests. Somebody might tell the invaders about her, of course, but maybe not.

Then again, staying here wouldn't help things. Mitch could be dead or wounded—she'd seen bodies being spaced last time she'd tried the monitors. Sooner or later she'd have to find water and food.

If they didn't know about her, she might be able to do something to help. The ship's ventilation system was big enough in places for her to move through it. She had experience in hiding, from when she was a kid and the aliens had taken over the colony. If you were quiet and quick, you could survive. She'd done it before.

And she had to find out what happened to Mitch. If he had been killed, then nothing mattered anymore. If he was still alive, she could find out, could do something to help him.

She stood. Yes. She wasn't going to spend whatever remained of her life cowering in the darkness waiting to be found and eliminated like some vermin. At the very least she could go down fighting.

In the APC bay, Massey and Wilks watched the landing craft being loaded. The marines were herded into the vessel by the guards, all of whom were androids.

"You'll stay here," Massey said to Wilks.

"Why?"

"Because I wish it so. We have enough worms for our hooks."

"You're sending my men to be slaughtered."

"Yes. But my forces will cover them from the air pods as best they can. They're already down there, buzzing around, setting up cover patterns. Live bait works better than dead, according to my information."

"Bastard."

"Not true. Both my parents stayed alive until I was nine. Then I killed them."

Wilks watched the squads marching onto the drop ship.

"The atmosphere is marginal down there," Massey said. "Little short on the oxy side, long on the CO_2 and other trash gases, got some methane and ammonia that'll probably make eyes burn and noses run. Extended exposure will be fatal, but I doubt anybody'll be there that long."

Wilks said nothing. They were in deep shit. The only bright spot seemed to be that Massey and his thugs hadn't found out about Billie. They would, eventually, when they strained enough of the ship's logs to get to Stephens's personal stuff. And she was probably on a monitor recording. Sooner or later somebody would ask the computer the right question and it would give them Billie.

He hoped she found a good place to hide and stayed there.

Inside the APC, Bueller sat at his station, waiting for the ship to drop. He'd been prepared to meet the aliens, but not like this, not unarmed and marched across the ground by enemies in air pods. They wouldn't have a prayer against those things, even if only half of what Wilks said was accurate.

Still, there was nothing to be done about it. A direct confrontation with the androids guarding them would mean a fast death. As long as they stayed alive, there was a chance they might be able to do something to survive.

He thought about Billie. He hoped she kept hidden. If he could be sure of that, then dying wasn't so bad.

Amazing that somebody like him could fall in
love. Amazing, but true enough.

The whine of the repellors cycling up and lifting
the ship free of the grapples for the drop interrupted
Bueller's thoughts. I love you, Billie, he said to
himself.

Good-bye.

Billie crawled through a stacked-plastic tube only
a few centimeters bigger than she was. It was hard,
slow, rough on her hands and arms as she dragged
herself along. But it wasn't as if she had a whole lot
of choice.

Wilks found himself in one of the forward store-
rooms alone, the door locked and guarded by a pair
of Massey's androids. Things didn't look good for
the home team.

Massey sat in front of the telemetry array, watching the feeds from the APC and helmetcams the
marines wore. The usual life-systems input wasn't
there. The Colonial Marines must be on a tight
budget these days. Well. That didn't matter. He
didn't care if they died, he only needed another
specimen or two and whatever information he could
gather on the aliens' homeworld. Plenty of that
coming in. The APC sensors gathered it up, gravity,
atmosphere, lighting, weather conditions, all kinds
of readings, and spewed it into the *Benedict*'s recor-
ders. Offhand, it didn't look like a world that was
going to become a vacation spot anytime soon.
Gravity a bit higher than Terran Standard, maybe a

gee and a quarter, so fat people and those with heart conditions would not like it much, even if it happened to look like Paradise, and in no way did it look inviting. The local star made most of the planet tropical, at least weather-wise. There were small ice caps at the poles, but even the more temperate regions would give you body heat plus a couple degrees. Vegetation was sparse, the oceans were full of nasty salts, and there didn't seem to be many places where an unprotected human could survive even *without* killer locals prowling for supper. The poisoned air would require full-time filters or implants. Looked like a place to dump garbage to Massey.

"Commander, we are breaking through the overcast, " came the android pilot's voice.

"I hear you."

Massey switched to the nose cam in the APC. The hologram lit the air to his left, showing a swirl of clouds that flew past and thinned. Under the cloud cover, the land below was dull and gray, scraggly trees or what passed for them, lots of young igneous rock exposed to the air, sharp edges, and dirty colors.

"Got a big thunderstorm forty klicks ahead," the copilot said. "Tops up to twenty thousand meters, look at the voltage on that lightning."

"Go around the storm," Massey ordered. "Find me a nest of the things and put down within a couple of kilometers. Don't want our marines to get too tired on their walk."

"Copy, Commander."

Massey watched the shifting pictures. So far, this

mission had gone exactly as he had planned. Right on the nose. It was almost boring. Maybe something would happen down there to spice things up a little.

Billie found that the ventilation tube opened into one of the small kitchens. Nobody seemed to be around, so she slid down the shaft and wiggled her way onto a microwave oven top. She quickly climbed to the floor.

Most of the food preparation on the *Benedict* consisted of heating and opening SMPs. That didn't require anything more than pulling and twisting a tab. Nobody produced wonderful meals for dinner here, but there were some special occasions when something a bit more elaborate than field rations might be called for. Visiting officers, an ambassador, perhaps. So the kitchen could be used to make a soypro cutlet or a stew, maybe even a pie or cake, and therefore there were implements.

Billie dug through all the cabinets until she found a combination knife and vegetable peeler with a U-shaped slotted extrusion pointed for coring. The edges were serrated on one side and sharp on the other; the blade was only as long as her forefinger. Not much of a weapon, but she could stab somebody with it if she could get close enough.

A better find was a tapered hollow plastic tube that could be filled with liquid and frozen, to make a rolling pin. Billie triggered the freezer in the handle and in about twenty seconds the liquid inside turned solid. It was cold in her grip but heavy and solid; she could bash in a skull with it. Again, it wasn't as good as a gun, but it was better than nothing.

She hefted the rolling pin. Now all she had to do was sneak up behind a whole shipful of armed men and whack each one on the head. Simple, right?

She chuckled to herself. You've lost your mind for sure this time, kid. Still, it felt better to be doing *some*thing.

Massey watched from the remote hovercam as the marines marched out onto the surface of the alien world, in full gear except for weapons. Six of his own troops floated in three small open-air pod craft over the walking marines. The androids in the pods were armed and the marines below knew they could either do as they were told or be cut down.

Sensors watched and listened and smelled and tasted and fed the results to Massey. He monitored his androids as they spoke to each other on their coms.

"—move pretty well for men who don't have enough oxygen to breathe—"

"—we in jeopardy here?"

"That's a negative, the alien life form is ground-based."

Massey mentally tuned out the chatter. His plan was simple enough: he would march the marines into the nearest hive where the aliens could grab them and implant eggs in them. Then he would send his androids in to retrieve them. Stephens had been instructed to refuse to allow plasma rifles on his ship, but Massey had enough such weapons and chargers on the company vessel to outfit a small army. However tough the aliens might be, they couldn't stand up to energy blasts that would blow holes in durasteel armor plate easier than a man could poke his finger through damp tissue paper. No, that wasn't going to be a problem. Once he had a specimen or two and all the information he could collect, he would head back to Earth.

Maybe after that the company could find him something *difficult* to do.

He laughed aloud. It was tough being the best. You had to invent your own challenges. Maybe he would quit the company, go to work for some smaller, hungrier concern. Turn against the people who now fed him and bite their hand a few times, just to show them he could do it. Yes. That had a certain appeal to it.

Ah, well. Best not to get too overconfident. One mission at a time. You didn't get to be the best by making mistakes, and counting embryos before the eggs were fertilized was unwise. He turned back to the holograms and information flow in front of him. One mission at a time.

20

Bueller and 1st Squad approached the mound cautiously—unarmed as they were, and walking knowingly to their deaths. The mound—nest? hive? whatever—loomed like an apartment-building-sized anthill. The surface was ridged and convoluted, a dull blackish-gray with bits of lighter color here and there. As they drew nearer, Bueller saw that the lighter bits were bones, a lot of them skulls, all blended into the surface.

"Damn," somebody said quietly.

"Some kind of secretion, all right, with a little organic stuff mixed in for the hell of it."

There was an oval-shaped entrance with a beaten path leading to it maybe a hundred meters ahead.

"I ain't going in there," Ramirez said. "Fuck this."

But the trio of air pods buzzing back and forth

overhead like dragonflies meant otherwise. As if to confirm this, Bueller's com came to life. "Move in," the voice said. And to punctuate the command, a thin green plasma beam splashed against the ground behind the squad, digging a small smoking crater into the stony surface.

"Wonder how the other squads are doing?" Chin said.

"Who cares?" Ramirez said. "We're about to become history here."

"This is what we came for," Bueller said.

"Fuck that," Ramirez said. "We are supposed to be marines, not bait!"

"I'm open to other ideas," Bueller said.

The six of them moved toward the entrance of the mound. Once they were inside the place, maybe they could just squat down and not go in any deeper.

Right, Bueller. And the guy on the monitor'll go blind and not see from our cams that we're standing still.

So, what can they do about it?

They can fry us with a reflected plasma beam, that's what they can do about it.

Oh, yeah. Right.

Or they can send one of the expendable androids down to hose us. Probably won't even have to get out of the air pod. Like Ramirez said, we're history.

The group reached the entrance. Bueller flicked his shoulder light on and took a deep breath. He stepped into the mound first.

Whatever was gonna happen was gonna happen.

* * *

Billie wound her way slowly from the kitchen to the hallway that led toward the ship's armory. A rolling pin and a peeler weren't going to get her very far against a shipful of armed men. She needed a gun. And a whole lot of good luck. Maybe even a miracle or two.

Massey was staring through the holographic readouts when a tiny chime called for his attention. He focused on the screen. The three air pods were holding over the entrance to the first mound; the other marine squads hadn't made it to their destinations yet. What was—?

Doppler showed aircraft closing on the air pods.

Impossible! There wasn't any civilization on this world. The aliens didn't have, couldn't have flying devices!

Then he realized what was wrong with the images. No heat signatures, no power leakage, no radio or radar or Doppler. Either the craft were so primitive they had to be gliders, or . . .

Massey blinked. "Team One," he said. "Alert!"

The first wave of flying creatures dived on the air pods. The cameras caught and recorded the images. They looked reptilian, with grayish, scaled skin. They had delta-shaped wings that spanned at least ten meters, short, sleek bodies and elongated heads with rows of pointed teeth. Carnivores, definitely. There were a dozen in the first group and they attacked soundlessly the three pods.

The androids were good, Massey had to give them that. The plasma rifles lit and lines of green swept

the air. The creatures fell and died as the high-
energy beams cut off wings, slashed bodies, lopped
heads. Nine of the things went down in the first
three seconds as the six androids fired their weapons repeatedly, dodging in the agile little pods.

But the second wave arrived and there were too
many. One of the things took a beam in the chest,
was probably dead instantly, but slammed into a
pod and knocked it sideways. Another attacker flew
in while the pod was tumbling and showed how
well those big toothy jaws worked when it bit an
arm from one of the androids. The one flying the
pod. The pod spiraled down toward the ground, four
or five of the beasts following it in controlled dives.

The other two pods were also in trouble. Flapping
wings buffeted the androids as the things darted in
and snapped at the heavy plastic, tore at it with
taloned claws as if the pods were themselves alive.

Plasma beams flashed, the flying monsters died
under the flares of energy, but those who weren't
hit kept attacking. One of the pods looked like a
popcorn ball beset by a flock of starving crows; the
plastic was pocked with gouges and bite marks,
dented from impacts. The androids fought on, but
they were losing.

The first pod splatted against the ground, shattered, and hurled the two androids away from the
impact. Almost instantly the flying creatures were
upon the androids, tearing at them, ripping limbs
from torsos, spraying circulating fluid up in thin
white fountains.

They tore the androids apart but didn't eat them.

Apparently they didn't much like the taste of artificial flesh.

Massey watched, amazed, as one of the pods landed in a controlled dive and one of the androids leapt out and sprinted toward the mound. While the flying animals fell on the other android still trying to exit the pod, they did not pursue the fleeing one. They must have known what the aliens in the mounds were capable of. The running android neared the entrance.

The third pod burst into flame while still thirty meters above the ground. By the time it crashed, both the passengers inside had been mostly consumed in the fire. One of the plasma rifles went critical in the heat and a blinding green flash turned the pod into dust, along with four or five of the attackers who had followed it down too closely.

How interesting, Massey thought. Surely there was a market for these things. Perhaps he could capture one. A baby, perhaps.

But first, he had to protect his primary mission. He called the pods shepherding the other marines. "Go immediately to the 1st Squad coordinates," he said.

"What about the marines here?" one of the androids asked.

"Who cares? Do as I order. Keep a ground-hugging flight path. There are flying aliens here who will attack you. Get moving."

He broke the com and leaned back in his form-chair. Yes. This was turning out to be more interesting than he had anticipated.

*   *   *

Bueller heard the explosion and stopped.

"What the hell?" Chin began.

They were only fifty or sixty meters into the nest and the devil they knew suddenly seemed less dangerous than the one they didn't. "Let's go see," Bueller said.

"I'm with you, pal," Ramirez said.

"I'll watch our rear," Mbutu said. She held a fist-sized rock in her hand. She waved the rock.

Bueller had to laugh. Mbutu was crazy if she thought a rock was going to do her any good. Then again, any weapon was better than none. Bueller looked around for a stone of his own. Better to go down trying than not.

What they saw was amazing. There were some kind of flying things flapping around like giant bats out there. All three pods were down, only one of them intact, and one of the androids was hauling ass toward the mound, moving at Olympic speed as he broken-stepped the rugged ground. He carried a plasma rifle in one hand.

"Move back," Bueller said. "I think maybe some luck just went our way."

"Maybe," Smith said from behind him. "What I want to know is how come the things who live here haven't swarmed all over us by now."

"Don't look a gift horse in the mouth," Chin said.

"What does that mean?"

"It means be glad you're still sucking in the air," Chin said. "Such that it is."

They watched the android run. One of the flying things made a half hearted pass at him, swooping down like a giant raptor seeking prey, but the

android dived flat and the thing missed by ten
meters anyhow. By the time it circled around for
another try, the android was nearly at the mound's
entrance. The flying thing must have decided it had
business elsewhere. It soared upward, caught a
thermal, and lifted away.

"Get ready for company," Bueller said.

The android reached the entrance and ran inside.
He never had a chance. All six of the marines hit
him, and he sprawled under their combined weight,
helpless.

Now they had a weapon. It wasn't much, but it
sure beat the alternatives.

Billie returned to the armory where she and
Mitch had been only a few hours past. There were
weapons aplenty, but after examining several of
them, she realized that they were all missing the
same part. She mentally shrugged, and slung one
of the carbines over her shoulder, collected a couple
of spare magazines and a flexbelt of grenades.
Maybe she could find the part to fix it. Or maybe
she could bluff somebody into thinking it was work-
able. Or threaten to blow up the ship with a grenade. If she was up against it and going to die
anyway, what the hell, she'd have nothing to lose.

Especially if something had happened to Mitch.

Bueller said, "All right. Blake, you're the best shot
in the squad, you get the plasma rifle."

She nodded, took the weapon, and did a quick
inspection. "Got almost full charge," she said.
"Thirty, thirty-five shots."

"If you have to use them, make them count," Bueller said.

"He's got a sidearm, too." That from Smith.

"Better let me have it," Bueller said.

"No offense, Bueller, but who died and left you in charge? We're all the same rank here since Easley bought it."

"I outscored everybody in pistol qualification."

"Yeah, Smith," Mbutu said, "you couldn't hit a tank at arm's length with a sidearm."

"Yeah, well, okay, fine," Smith said. "I was just checking, you know."

Bueller took the pistol, a standard 10mm caseless slug thrower. It used ammunition close to that of the carbines, except it was less powerful, and in a pinch could be made to fire the heavier stuff—if you didn't mind risking that the pistol would most likely blow up after five or six shots.

"Okay, pal," Bueller said to the captured android, "let's you and us talk."

"Wasting your time," the android said. "I'm no good as a hostage, I'm expendable, and my clock is running down. I'm dead in a couple weeks no matter what."

"You could have a real miserable couple of weeks, though," Mbutu said, hefting her rock.

The android shook its head. "I don't know anything, either. Massey runs the show and he keeps it to himself. We get what he wants us to get, nothing more."

Blake kicked the pinned android, hitting his hip with her boot. "Fine," she said. "Let's kill him now.

Go ahead, Mbutu, bust his head with your rock, no point in wasting a bullet or a charge on him."

"Ease off, Blake," Bueller said. "This guy came out of the vats and got programmed for this. It's not his fault. Not everybody gets a choice."

Blake stared at Bueller. "Yeah. I guess I hear that."

"I hate to point this out, but *I* hear something coming this way from inside the nest," Smith said. "And even a plasma rifle won't stop a whole herd of these bugs. What say we go play outside?"

Bueller glanced down the corridor. He heard the rattle of alien feet and claws on the material. "Let's move it, people. Get to the downed pods, there might be more guns or supplies, something."

"And then go where?" the android asked. "You're trapped on the planet without pods or an APC."

"Maybe so, pal, but we *ain't* trapped in this ant-hill. Let's go, marines."

Nobody needed to be told again.

Billie moved carefully through the ship, hiding when she heard people approaching. She had the carbine over her shoulder and clutched the rolling pin and peeler in her hands. She kept moving away from the voices and bootfalls until she realized she was in the ship's crew and commanding officer's quarters. She snaked her way around doorways and stayed flat against the walls, edging along, trying to stay invisible. If somebody should see her, she would be in deep shit in a real hurry.

Ahead was Stephens's cabin, and something drew Billie that way. He wouldn't be using it—one of the bodies she'd seen spaced had been the colonel. Surprised her, that he would die defending the ship, but maybe she'd read him wrong.

As Billie approached the door, it started to open.

Damn, somebody was inside!

She glanced up and down the corridor. She'd never get clear in time. Whoever came out of Stephens's cabin would see her before she could get to cover. If he was armed, she'd catch one in the back.

Billie raised the rolling pin, triggered the freezer, and flattened herself against the wall to the right of the sliding door. She hoped it was only one of them.

As the man stepped out into the corridor, Billie swung the rolling pin. The liquid inside hadn't solidified yet, but the pin was still heavy.

She smashed the pin into the man's head, angled just over his left ear. She put her shoulder and back into it, it was a good swing, powered further by her fear. The thick plastic shattered as it met bone, probably cracking the skull as well. Viscous blue coolant splashed from the broken pin, covering the man's face with cold globules.

He didn't go down. He staggered, slammed into the doorjamb, and wobbled, but he didn't go down.

Billie stepped in and drove her left hand at the man's belly, just below the sternum. The peeler sank into his flesh all the way to her hand.

White fluid sprayed from the wound onto her as she jerked the peeler out.

Android blood, she realized, as she tried for the second stab. He was an artificial person.

The android managed to twist and slap at her hand, partially deflecting the second thrust so it missed his solar plexus and skidded over his ribs, gouging chunks of his uniform and flesh out, leaving a shallow ditch that stretched from the center of his chest almost to his shoulder.

The coolant from the rolling pin clouded his vision, though, and his own punch missed Billie by a hair. As he wiped at his eyes, it gave Billie enough time for one more shot. If she didn't drop him with it, he would have her. Even a wounded android was still stronger than an ordinary human.

Billie jabbed, a long stroke, aiming at his eye. Growing up in a hospital you learned something about anatomy. The eyes were the easiest path through the skull to the brain.

The peeler hit just under her target, bounced up, and sank through the softer eye tissue. Jelly oozed from the ruined eye as the peeler went in.

The android jerked away from Billie, reached up with both hands, and jerked the peeler out. The serrated edge brought most of the eye out with it, clearing the socket until milky white circulating fluid welled and spilled.

He stood here for what seemed a long time, then collapsed. He didn't say anything, not even a groan, just dropped as if his bones had vanished, and died.

Billie's heart raced, pounding as though trying to dig its way out of her body. She still held part of the shattered rolling pin in her right hand. She let it fall. The clatter it made seemed loud in the corridor.

Her first reaction was to turn and run, but she didn't. Instead, she wondered why the android had been in Stephens's cabin.

Inside, she figured it out. The parts missing from

the carbines were stacked neatly in rows on the colonel's bed. Who would have put them there? Somebody had sabotaged the weapons, and it looked like she had found out who. Why had he done it? It didn't matter, she could worry about that later. Right now, she had other things on her mind.

Billie picked up one of the feed ramps, stripped the receiver on her weapon, and replaced the missing part. She snapped the connector into place and the ramp toggled through a diagnostic code and then clicked into place. She shoved a magazine into the carbine, touched the bolt control, and cycled a round into the firing chamber. The magazine's counter showed ninety-nine antipersonnel rounds remaining.

Billie smiled. It was tight, but she felt a lot better. If the headshrinkers in the clinic could see her now, they'd really have something to worry about: good God, it's a crazy woman with a gun!

Damn straight. And if anybody gave her any shit, she was going to invite them onto the dance floor for a fast and deadly tattoo tango.

Wilks. She would go find Wilks and get him loose. He'd know how to handle this. And once she got Wilks, they could collect Mitch and get the hell out of this mess. Maybe it wasn't the best plan in the universe, but it would do for now.

She hoped.

21

Massey watched as the other six air pods arrived in the vicinity of the 1st Squad's hive.

Watched the various angles the cameras gave him as the marines began shooting the pods out of the sky.

Well, well. They must have gotten hold of some of the downed weaponry. At least two plasma rifles were working from the ground, spearing his troops with brilliant green spikes.

His androids were pretty good, but they were general-purpose expendables, strong and quick, not extensively trained for formal combat scenarios. In this kind of thing the marines had the edge, even though they weren't armed very well. Three of the six pods flamed out and crashed; the other three quickly pulled out of range and hovered over the area.

"Commander," came the query from the com, "we have a problem here."

"I'm not blind," Massey said. "Hold your position. Keep them in sight."

He leaned back in his chair and rubbed at his chin. He turned away and called to the android standing guard at the door. "Go get Wilks and bring him here."

The android left.

Hmm. Yes, this was much more challenging than he had expected. Still, it was a minor setback. He had uploaded a raft of information about the planet, and his primary mission, to keep the government from securing an alien specimen, was accomplished. Should he continue this, or cut his losses and go home? On the one hand, he'd done pretty much what they wanted him to do—he could tell the company that the surface teams had been destroyed by alien wildlife and they would shrug it off as nothing. The company had its specimen, another one would only be backup. On the other hand, he hated the idea of even a partial failure.

Yes, it was an interesting question. He'd have to think about it a little more.

It was blind luck that let Billie see the pirate moving Wilks along, a gun jammed into the marine's back. Wilks had his hands crossed behind him and held with a thin carbon-fiber cuffstrip. The man—or was it another android?—herding Wilks along didn't glance down the corridor as he passed, his attention being on his prisoner, so he didn't see Billie crouched down by a radiator heat sink.

When they had gone by, Billie stood and cat-footed to the end of the cross corridor. She peeped around the corner in time to see them turn toward the control deck. Well, she had wanted to find Wilks and now she had. She slipped into the main corridor and started after the two.

Wilks had a feeling that wherever he was going, he might not be leaving under his own power. What the hell, he figured. He'd been living on borrowed time for more than a decade. He should have died with his squad back on Rim. It had all been gravy since, and not real tasty most of the time anyhow. Fuck it. If his number was up, then his number was up. He was going to go down like a man.

Bueller had the squad dispersed and shifting positions every few seconds. They were lucky the air pods hadn't been designed for anything other than quick and dirty transportation—the little craft didn't have much in the way of sensing gear, only basic radar and Doppler, no sniffers or IR. And no weapons except what the passengers themselves carried. Since the androids flying the pods had to rely on their own senses for targeting, the camo suits the marines wore made it difficult to see them. *They* were hard to see but the *pods* weren't. And the two plasma rifles the squad had would reach the same distance as the ones in the pods. So if they came down within range to splash the marines, they risked getting smoked themselves. And since they were much bigger and better targets, so far the score was marines three, pirates nada.

Then again, they couldn't sit here on the ground much longer. Sooner or later the bugs would come swarming out of the mound and that would make things more than a little worse for the squad. They couldn't afford to be pinned down here.

"Okay, everybody listen up," Bueller said, using his scrambled opchan. "We got to move out before company comes looking for dinner, everybody copy? On my signal, we rocket, magnetic south. Ramirez, you take point, Blake you cover. Everybody else keep your head down and give me asses and elbows."

Bueller didn't think the pirates could tap their opchan, but he remembered the lesson he'd learned from Wilks when he and Easley had gotten nailed during a practice assault back on Earth. "On my signal, marines, gainsay prior."

The last was a code. It meant move at 180 degrees to the last order. If the pirates *did* have an ear tuned to their private line, they'd be looking for the marines to move south. The squad would be going north, however, and it might buy them a few hundred more meters.

"Go!"

The captured android had been listening to Bueller give the order. Bueller didn't think about it until they were moving—the android didn't know their codes. When the marines scrambled, the pirate android went the wrong way.

"Hey!" Bueller yelled.

Too late. One of the pods swooped down to the
south of their position, a plasma rifle on full auto.
Its charge wouldn't last long firing that way, but
hosing could cause a lot of damage in a short time.
The ground smoked and cratered; rocks screamed
as they shattered under the blasts of energy; the
pirate android tried to stop but ran into the dancing
lines of green death. His internal fluids boiled and
he exploded like a water balloon stuck with a sharp
knife. Well, it was quick. He wouldn't have suffered
much.

Blake pulled up, spun, and sighted at the pod.
The craft looped from its dive and started to lift.

"Too far," Bueller yelled. "Don't waste your shot!"

Blake grinned, her smile wide. She kept both
eyes open as she aimed, followed the pod with her
rifle, then squeezed off the plasma bolt.

It was five hundred meters if it was a centimeter,
a fast-moving target. Not much chance of hitting it,
Bueller thought.

The green beam drilled the pod dead center. The
energy bolt coruscated against the heavy plastic,
ate its way through in less time than it took a
nervous man to blink, and burned out the pod's
repellors. The pod seemed to hang motionless for a
heartbeat, suspended in time and space, then it fell
like a fat lead ball dropped in heavy gravity. Without
the repellor, an air pod had the aerodynamics of a
round brick. They were close enough to hear the
atmosphere whistle across the hole the plasma bolt
made. The thing hit the ground hard enough to
make the hard dirt splash.

"Nice shot," Bueller said.

"Like duck hunting," she said. "Got to lead the target a little, that's all."

They ran.

The remaining two pods circled high overhead, keeping well out of range.

"Where are we going?" Chin yelled.

"To the APC."

"It's the other way!"

"I know. We'll circle around. Let them think we're lost. Once it gets dark we can lose these slush-brains."

"Yeah," Mbutu said, "but can we lose *them*?"

Behind the running marines, aliens began to emerge from the nest.

Massey dismissed the android. He turned to Wilks and said, "Your marines have proven quite adept down there. Seems they managed to get their hands on a couple of weapons and now they're making a run for it."

Wilks grinned. "That's too bad. I hope that hasn't upset your little plan any."

Massey pulled his antique pistol from its holster and stuck it under Wilks's chin, shoving the barrel into his flesh. "Here's an idea: Why don't you call them and tell them to surrender?"

Wilks managed to grin even wider. "You gonna do what, *kill* me if I don't?"

Massey laughed, backed off a little with the pistol. "It's nice to work with professionals after all the scum I usually have to deal with. You know I'm going to kill you no matter what."

"I sort of suspected that."

"It's necessary, you know. But you can go hard or you can go easy." Massey holstered the gun and pulled a thin boot knife. The stainless steel glittered in the overhead lights. The knife was only about seventeen or eighteen centimeters long, half of that handle, but it didn't take much in the hands of an expert. Wilks didn't doubt that Massey knew how to use it.

"Hell, my dick is bigger than that," Wilks said.

"Not for long."

Wilks gathered himself. His hands were bound behind him, but he could use his feet. Doubtless Massey knew hand-to-hand, but better to die trying than not.

The com chimed.

Massey moved back, outside of Wilks's range, and touched a control. "Commander, the marines have shot down another of our pods. They are moving north, away from the APC coordinates."

"They aren't that stupid," Massey said. "Stay with them. Targets of opportunity." He glanced at Wilks, then back at the com. He touched other controls on the board. A timer lit the air in one corner of the standard screen projection. It began to count down.

"Better safe than sorry," he said.

Wilks went for it. He took a couple of quick steps toward Massey.

Massey laughed and snapped up a sidekick. The move was almost lazy, a contemptuous strike. His boot caught Wilks in the belly and knocked him down. He hit hard, unable to use his hands to break his fall. He dug with his heels in a futile effort to get up. He'd never make it.

Massey twirled the knife in his hand. "This game is being called on account of rain," he said. "Time to take my winnings and go home. So long, Sergeant Wilks." He started toward the helpless marine.

"Drop it!" came a woman's voice from behind Massey.

Evening threw long shadows over the alien landscape, and as the sun settled for the night, Bueller and his squad started their circle toward the APC. It was harder to see the air pods trailing them, and therefore it would be harder for the pirates to see them, too.

"What about the aliens?" Bueller asked.

Mbutu shook her head. "They must have lousy senses of smell," she said. "When we cut left back there, they kept going straight. Crummy trackers."

"That's good."

"Maybe," Ramirez said. "Or maybe there's something in this direction they don't want to run into. Something meaner than they are."

"That's what I like about you, Ramirez, you always look on the bright side of things," Blake said.

"Fuck you, Blake."

"You wish. If you had anything bigger than a toothpick I might consider it."

Bueller grinned. They might all die out here, but if they could make jokes, then morale was higher than it had been since the pirates had boarded them.

"Let's hustle it up, marines. We got places to go and things to do."

*   *   *

Billie had the carbine aimed at the pirate's heart and if he made any sudden moves she was going to carve it out of him.

The man grinned as he let the knife fall. He looked like some of the psychotics Billie had seen in the lockdown section of the hospital.

"Well, well. What have we here? You the ship's mascot?"

"Stay real still."

"So that explains the extra on the head count. You can't be one of those ugly marines, you're too pretty. Crew smuggle you onboard for fun and games, maybe?"

Wilks said, "Shoot him, Billie. Shoot him now!"

The man glanced at Wilks. "Ah. Friend of yours, eh, Sergeant? You have nice taste." He turned back toward Billie. Slid a half step toward her, hands outstretched wide, trying to look harmless.

"Another step and I punch your ticket," she said.

"Come on. Sweet little thing like you? You don't want to kill me. Think about what it would be like, being responsible for the death of another human being. It'll give you bad dreams, honey." He slid another half step forward.

Billie swallowed, her mouth dry. This man was a killer, she had seen the bodies get spaced. And he had done something with Mitch. But his hands were in the air. Shooting somebody down like this, it was different from thunking the android on the head.

Billie shuffled back a step. "I'm telling you to stop right there."

Wilks managed to lever himself to his feet by leaning against a bulkhead. "Billie, this guy is a murderer! You have to put him down! Shoot!"

She glanced at Wilks.

A mistake.

As soon as her attention left the pirate, he leapt. God, he was fast! Billie pulled the trigger on the carbine, but he was already twisting, dropping under the line of her fire. Half a dozen rounds shattered a computer console, the noise was awful, lights flickered as the power surged and shorted in the plugged console—

She tried to realign the weapon but too late. He hit her above the knees, and she did a half flip forward and landed on her back—

"Stupid bitch!" he said as he rolled up and caught Billie by the shoulders. "Point a goddamn gun at me!" He snatched her from the floor and threw her against the bulkhead.

Billie went gray as her head slammed against the wall. Even as she bounced off, he was on her, one hand grabbing her shirt, the other slapping her face. "I don't need a weapon, you stupid cunt, I could tear your throat out with my fingers!" He slapped her again. Billie felt a tooth cut the inside of her lip. Blood sprayed from her mouth as he slapped her the third time. He shoved her back against the wall, lifted her feet clear of the deck by her shirt. Pulled his pistol from his holster. Grinned like a maniac.

"But I don't dirty my hands on nothings like you."

As he raised the gun to kill her, Billie saw a blur behind him. She couldn't stop her gasp.

The pirate tried to turn, but she locked both her hands around the wrist of the hand he held her with. It slowed him enough so that Wilks hit him with one shoulder just above his hip. Billie felt her shirt tear as the pirate was knocked away.

She fell to the floor and scrabbled on all fours.

Toward the carbine where it had fallen. Five meters. Four. Three—

The pirate roared and Billie twisted enough to see him. He had lost his pistol, but he was up and diving for it.

Two meters to the carbine. One—

"I'll kill both of you!"

Wilks was sprawled on his side, pushing himself along with only his left foot. Toward the pirate.

Billie reached the carbine. Grabbed it. Rolled onto her back. Wouldn't be time to get to her feet—

The pirate's gun went off, but she was rolling and she felt the slug hit the deck where she had just been. No time to aim. She pushed the gun out as if it were her fist punching and pulled the trigger. The fire selector must have been jiggled when the gun had fallen. It went off once. Billie, expecting full auto, couldn't figure it out. She held the trigger back, waiting for more fire. Nothing. She'd have to let it go and pull it again, she realized. Oh, fuck!

But one was enough.

The caseless 10mm round caught the pirate just below the shoulder of his gun arm. Blew a hole through him. Billie saw him tumble, the gun falling from his nerveless fingers. The entry wound was the size of her fingertip, but when he fell she saw the exit wound, high on his back, was as big as her fist.

The pistol slid two meters away from the fallen man's fingertips. He raised his head, saw the pistol, crawled for it. Stretched his good hand out for it.

Billie came up, carbine held ready, and jumped for the pistol. Kicked it across the room. Pointed the carbine at the downed man.

He rolled over onto his back. Blood poured from his wound, spreading under his head in a coppery-smelling pool.

"Stupid fucking bitch," he said. He reached for something at his waist.

"Don't move!"

"Fuck you." He slid his left hand into a vertical slit on his coverall over his right hip. She saw him smile as he gripped it.

"Billie!" Wilks yelled.

"Stop!" she screamed.

He started to pull his hand out—

She squeezed the trigger.

The explosion was loud in the enclosed room, it lapped against the hard walls and splashed back at her. The smell of burnt propellant filled her nostrils. Her ears rang.

The round hit him square in the mouth. Chopped out some front teeth and blew the back of his head all over the deck and wall behind him. Whatever he had intended to do wasn't ever going to happen.

She bent, tugged his hand out. He death-gripped a grenade. The safety cap had already been snapped up and his thumb was on the detonate button. Carefully, Billie pried the grenade loose from the dead man's hand and closed the safety cap. He would have blown them all up, ruined the control room, sent the ship spiraling down to burn in the atmosphere.

"Billie, cut me lose."

She looked at Wilks, blinked as if she'd never seen him before. "What?"

"He's set some kind of timer going. Hurry!"

Numbly, Billie obeyed. She found the fallen knife, used it to cut the strand binding Wilks. The knife was very sharp.

Free, Wilks ran to the com board. Looked at the screen. A bullet had shattered the projector. He couldn't see how much time was left. He started tapping controls on the console, swore, then moved to another screen.

"What is it?"

He shook his head. "I think it's a bomb set on the APC. 1st Squad got loose. He was afraid they'd get to the APC and come back."

"What about Mitch?"

"I don't know."

"Call him! Find out!"

"Billie—"

"Goddammit, Wilks!"

"Let me see if I can stop this timer. They'll need a way off the planet. Go guard the door! There are still a couple of the androids running around loose!"

She stared at him.

"Go, do it! If they get us, we all die!"

Billie moved. She pushed the selector to full auto, looked out into the corridor, didn't see anybody. She stood at the doorway, watching.

"Wilks?"

"I don't have enough time! There's got to be a failsafe, a break-off command but I don't know the code. I'm trying to bust the APC controls open to shut the power down, maybe the destruct is run off of its systems. It's all I can do."

"How long?"

He shrugged. "Could be a minute, could be an hour. I can't tell. The system won't access it from here."

Billie turned back to watch the corridor. If Mitch was alive, she'd go down and find him. If not, then it didn't much matter.

"Damn!" Wilks said. "Damn, damn, damn!"

22

Fortunately for the squad they'd been issued IR viewers. The pirates had known the marines would be going into a dark hive, so they let them keep their red eyes.

So they could move in the dark.

The air pods might be buzzing around up there somewhere, but for now, the marines were better equipped and effectively invisible.

They approached the APC in the moonless night, guided by the landing craft's heat leaks. Ramirez had the point; he was several hundred meters ahead of the rest of them. Bueller had told Ramirez to pull up short, scout the area, and then report back. It was likely that there were guards on the lander and Bueller had to figure a way to take them out without damaging the craft.

Bueller was looking away from the lander when all of a moment the night turned to blinding day.

"Shit!" he said. He flipped the IR flat screen up and turned, using his own vision.

The fireball from the APC was still spreading, dimmed somewhat and growing darker as it expanded outward and upward. They were far enough away so that the shock wave was fairly mild; it was like a hot wind, a sudden breeze off a desert at midday. Bueller dropped flat, but realized even as he did so that his reflexes were too slow. If it had been dangerous they'd already be past tense.

After a second pieces of wreckage began to patter down, some of it hit nearby, a solid *chunk!* as a heavy object dug into the rocky soil. A bit of flaming debris arced past, still climbing, and other burning shards fell like a holiday fireworks display, a hot rain that pocked the dirt and went dark or bounced and stayed lit even after coming to rest.

"Oh, *man!*" Chin said.

Bueller spoke into the com. "Ramirez? Respond." The opchan was quiet.

"*Adios*, Ramirez," Mbutu said.

Bueller stared at the smoking ruin ahead of them. Ramirez must have gotten caught in the explosion. Damn!

He was sorry to lose Ramirez, but another cold fact lay in his belly like a bar of dry ice: with the APC destroyed, they were all fucked. End of mission. End of squad.

Damn.

* * *

Billie said to Wilks, "Can you contact the marines?"

The com board was alive with incoming calls, but all of them from the pirate androids, who were stranded on-planet when the APC blew. Wilks waved his hand over the cutoff control and the board fell silent. He touched another control.

"Fox Platoon, this is Sergeant Wilks. Anybody copy?"

For what seemed a long time to Billie there was no response. Oh, gods, Mitch!

"This is Bueller, 1st Squad."

"Mitch!"

Wilks waved her to silence. "Bueller, what's your situation?"

"I've got Blake, Smith, Chin, and Mbutu. We lost Ramirez when the APC went nova. How are things there?"

"Billie got the drop on the head bad guy. He's no longer with us. There are probably some of his troops still loose on the ship but we're armed and in the control center. I think we can clean them out okay."

"Interesting that his androids aren't First-Lawed," Bueller said.

"Yeah, ain't it, though. Listen up. I'll light the other APC and come down after your squad. This mission is going to be an abort, Bueller. The bad guys already have one of the bugs back home. Once the government hears that, they'll grab it. We don't need a specimen anymore."

"Copy that, Sergeant Wilks. We'll find a safe place for the APC to land—"

Suddenly a voice cut in over that of Bueller's, bleeding across a wide spectrum of the radio band.

"Help, somebody help! This is Walters, Second Officer. The androids put us down next to one of those fucking anthills and the things are coming out right toward us! Help us!"

Wilks said, "Dammit!" He fiddled with the com controls. "Walters, this is Wilks! Where are you? Give me a transponder beacon!"

"Jesus and Buddha! They're all over us! No! Leave me alone! Aaahh!"

"The beacon, Walters, trigger the beacon!"

Billie stared at Wilks.

"There it is!" he said. "He managed to kick it on."

Billie shook her head. "The things will take them into the hive. They'll web them up in the egg room."

Wilks nodded. "Yeah. Even with the beacon, we can't get to them before they get implanted. They're dead men." He blew out a short sigh. "I'm gonna nuke the planet from breakaway orbit," he said. "At least it'll be quick. We've got enough hardware. While Stephens was bitching about the plasma rifles, I was moving bomb components past him disguised as spare parts. I can put a ring of fire down there that'll trigger a thousand volcanoes. Between them and the nukes, they'll scour the place like a sandblaster. Sterilize the whole fucking planet."

"Sergeant Wilks," came Mitch's voice. "We heard the distress signal. It's only a dozen klicks from here. We're on the way."

"Negative on that, mister. The mission is an

abort, repeat, it is an abort. You find a spot for the APC and wait for it to collect you. That's an order."

"Sergeant, you know we can't leave those men in there."

Wilks's jaw muscles danced as he ground his teeth together.

"We'll call for the APC when we get them out," Mitch said.

Billie didn't understand what was going on. "Mitch! This is Billie! You can't save the crew; they are as good as dead! Wait for the APC!"

"I—I can't explain it, Billie, but we can't just let them die."

"Dammit, Mitch! What is this, some kind of marine honor thing? They're gone! They might be breathing for a while longer but they're dead if they get implanted! We couldn't do anything for them even if you could get them out! It isn't worth the risk!"

"I'm sorry, Billie. I love you."

"Mitch!"

"Save your breath," Wilks said. "You can't stop them."

"Why?"

But Wilks had nothing to say.

"Anything from the other squads?" Chin asked.

"No," Bueller answered. "I expect if any of them made it and still have coms working we'll see them at the hive."

Smith shook his head. "Damn, I don't like this."

"Tell me about it," Bueller said.

They moved off through the night.

*   *   *

There were four of Massey's First-Law-less androids on the ship. Wilks and Billie found and killed them all.

"I don't understand," Billie said. "I didn't think androids could hurt people."

"Close," he said. "They modified Asimov's First Law of Robotics for androids. They can't *kill* a human or even stand by and *allow* a human to be killed without trying to help. Otherwise there couldn't be android surgeons; they wouldn't be able to hurt somebody a little to save them from a bigger hurt or death. Apparently nobody told this group. Massey's backing must be very high up in the scheme of things to have pulled that one off."

Wilks programmed the remaining military lander, as well as the one from Massey's ship. The company ship would hang in standby orbit in case it was needed; he could pilot it by remote from the planet. Massey had dropped the little pods with their crews in what was called snowball wrap—it burned off going down—but the pods couldn't reach escape velocity to make it back out of the gravity well.

"I'm going down with you," Billie said.

"Not a good idea. I'd rather have you on the ship."

"I don't much care what you want. I'm going."

Wilks looked at her, shook his head. He'd tried to warn her, tried to keep her from getting involved with Bueller. It hadn't worked. Now she was having to pay the price. The cost was steep. He hurt for her, but maybe it was the best way. Bueller and the others were probably history, no better off than those of their crew the monsters had dragged into their mound for baby food. None of the other squads had answered his calls. The mission was a fuckup from the first. Damn.

"All right. You can go." What else could he say?

The squad had a stroke of good luck. Just before dawn they happened on one of the air pods. The little vehicle must have run low on fuel and put down next to a stream to try to recharge the converters. It would take a long time for the stream's water to power up the flywheel batteries—the thing wasn't much bigger than a ditch and the current was slow-moving—but it was not as if the passengers had a lot of choice. Running dry of power at a hundred meters in the air would guarantee a landing nobody would walk away from.

Using her red eye, Blake spiked the two androids from two hundred meters out, one shot each.

"So, do I get a medal or something?"

"Sure, Blake. When we get back to Earth, I'll put you in for the Marksmanship Badge."

"Aw, I already got that one, Bueller. I was hoping for a Platinum Star, at least."

"What the hell, that, too," Bueller said.

They grinned at each other, but the expressions were tight, whistling-past-the-graveyard humor. Their chances of getting out of this alive were as slim as those of a spitball in a supernova.

But they were better off now. The pod held two more plasma rifles and chargers, a 10mm carbine, and two softslug pistols. Everybody was armed, a plasma weapon for everybody except Bueller, who took the carbine and a belt of grenades.

"How's the pod's charge?" Bueller asked.

"Almost dead," Smith answered. "It'll take sixteen hours at the stream's flow rate to give it enough to lift. Even then, two passengers would be reaching."

Bueller shrugged. "Let it keep charging. Maybe it'll be useful when we get back."

"'When'?" Smith said. "My, ain't you the optimist."

"Let's move out."

Dawn lit the eastern skies with the first reddish glimmers of day.

"'Red sky in the morning, sailors take warning,'" Smith said.

"We're marines," Bueller said. "Let the Navy worry about that shit."

They marched toward the alien mound.

As the APC fell from the *Benedict*'s belly into space, Billie held her breath. Outside the ship's faux gravity field, she and Wilks were suddenly weightless, and that cold, pit-of-the-stomach flutter made her want to throw up. She swallowed the bile that threatened to spew and took deep breaths through her nose. Mitch was down there and still alive. If they could get to the hive before he went inside, she could maybe stop him. If they were too late for that, then she would grab a gun and go in after him.

"How long?" she asked.

"If we're lucky, maybe an hour."

"And if we aren't lucky?"

"We've got to skip through the atmosphere at a bad angle to make the rendezvous," he said. "If we do it wrong we could fry inside this can."

"What happens to the planet if we die?"

"If I don't put in a call to the ship in six hours, the computer drops the atomics and heads for home. Anybody left down there had better get their affairs in order real quick."

Billie looked at Wilks.

"You know what those things can do where there's only a few of them," he said. "I'm not taking any chances on leaving a whole planet full of them lying around for some other poor sucker to stumble on."

She nodded. He was right. If they died, it was best to take the entire world with them. It was the only way to be sure.

"There's the entrance," Mbutu said. "What's the drill?"

"I'll take the point," Bueller said. "Move in after me in a two-and-two, Mbutu, you and Chin in front, Blake, you and Smith covering our asses. We have the signal from the transponder, we go straight to it, recover the crew, come straight out."

"Easy as falling down a grav-shaft," Smith said.

"You got a warped sense of humor," Blake said. "Somebody must have jiggled the tech's arm when he was installing your brain matrix."

"Fuck you," Smith said.

"If we get back to the ship, I'm all yours, lover."

"That's great, Blake," Mbutu said, "give him a reason to die quicker."

"Let's move in, marines. People need our help in there."

They were two hundred meters into the mound when the first wave of aliens came at them. A dozen of the things, moving impossibly fast, fangs bared, claws extended.

"Aim low!" Bueller ordered. "Take out their legs!"

He snapped off three three-round bursts, waving the carbine in a short arc to his left, leaving the center and right of the corridor clear.

Green beams flashed past him and burned limbs from bodies. Several of the things fell and skidded on the ridged floor and others tangled with them.

Bueller pulled the softslug pistol from his belt. The exterior armor would stop the handgun's rounds, but when the things opened their mouths to extend those toothed rods, he fired his sidearm into the openings. The softslugs tore through the tissue inside the heads very nicely, and the projectiles stayed inside the harder skulls, doing enough damage to be fatal. Rattled around like a mad bumblebee in a jar.

It was over in five seconds, and the twelve attacking aliens lay burned or shattered, smoke rising where the blood touched the hive. Not that something that acidic could really be called blood.

"Don't step in the liquid," Bueller ordered.

"Stuff's not eating into the floor much," Blake said.

"Makes sense that it wouldn't," Chin said.

"Wouldn't do to have holes burned in the building every time some drone cut its finger."

"We're still five hundred meters away from our quarry," Bueller said. "Let's move."

The APC bounced, the ride bone-jarring despite the seat restraints. The atmosphere was cloudy, and visibility was nil. Wilks hoped the computer controls knew what they were doing. The hull temperature was hot enough to melt silver and climbing. The belly, nose, and underwing tiles on the APC were designed to take a lot more friction than they were getting, but if the lander slewed too much one way or the other, the heat could be a problem. If the skin burned through, it could cause fatal damage to the occupants in a matter of a couple of seconds. At least it would be fast.

"A-a-ar-are w-w-we g-g-gonna m-make it?"

Wilks looked at Billie. His own voice chattered with the vibrations when he answered. "M-m-maybe."

Another wave of monsters clattered toward the squad, hissing as they moved. Bueller's carbine rumbled, a giant tearing heavy canvas, and the armor-piercing rounds punched through the bodies where they hit straight on, ricocheted off when they struck at an angle, making sparks like flint on steel.

Chin was right behind Bueller and his plasma rifle flared, the pulses making the walls glow with a sickly verdant gleam.

One of the things tumbled, legs seared off at the

knees. It skidded into Bueller, knocked him to the side against the wall.

Bueller slammed into the surface, his head protected by the helmet but his shoulder hit hard. The force of the impact twisted him so as he fell away he saw what happened to Chin as if watching it on a holoviewer in slow motion.

—The legless alien spun, scrabbled with its taloned hands, and slid in at Chin under his line of fire. Chin tried to lower his aim, but too late. The alien opened massive jaws and bit, latching on to Chin's thigh—

—Chin screamed. He slammed the butt of the plasma rifle uselessly at the thing's armored skull—

—Blake yelled, "Don't move!" and slid over a step to shoot the alien that had Chin in its teeth—

—The alien's legs were gone, but it still had its tail. It speared Chin's belly, jammed the pointed tail through him so it emerged between two ribs on his back. The ribs broke through the skin, showing splintered bones—

—Blake fired, hit the alien behind the hinge of its jaws. The thing convulsed and the teeth sheared through Chin's leg completely. For a second he stood there on one leg, the monster's tail helping him stay up. Then he fell—

—Smith moved in to tug at Chin, the thing's tail still through him, and another alien flew past Bueller, blocking for an instant his view. He managed to raise his weapon, even though it had all happened so fast he was still falling after his impact with the wall—

—Bueller fired. One of the slugs *spanged* off the

alien, knocked its head sideways so it looked straight at Bueller. The other two rounds missed the alien. One of them found Chin and blew the top of his head off—

—Smith was close to the alien. As it twisted back to find him, Smith fired. He was too close. The focuser on the end of the plasma rifle nearly touched the thing. The beam pierced the alien's armor, but it also partially splashed. The plasma sprayed and hit Smith in the face. It cooked the flesh, boiled his eyes into steam. He fell back as the alien collapsed on him, its acid blood spewing onto Smith, eating through his armor and body, stinking smoke rising in a hot blast—

—Bueller hit the floor. He heard the hums of more plasma beams, saw the reflected green on the walls, came to his feet . . .

The second wave was over, maybe twenty more of the things lay dead, but both Smith and Chin also gone.

That left only three of them to save the crew.

Bueller looked at Blake and Mbutu. They nodded at him. Without speaking, they started deeper into the hive.

23

A hard jolt shook the APC and it dropped in free-fall for a second. Billie felt a moment of nausea. She'd never done particularly well in zero gravity; her stomach always twisted in what felt like a continuous drop from a great height. Then the little ship's wings caught the atmosphere again, weight returned, and she swallowed as her belly recovered its composure.

"That's the worst of it," Wilks said. "We're on a long glide path to the place now. Might hit a few clouds on the way, get a little chop, but that's pretty much it."

Billie nodded, not speaking. Would it be too late? Would Mitch still be alive? As much as anybody, Billie knew the dangers of the enemies her lover faced. Whatever their motivation, they were killing machines, and if they cared about their own deaths, it never showed. Survival of the species was the thing; individuals didn't seem to matter much. Not like people. Not like people at all.

"How long?"

"Thirty minutes, give or take. We have to glide in so we'll have enough juice to achieve escape velocity and make it back to the ship."

Billie nodded again. There was not much to say about that.

There was a side passage to Bueller's left and he put thirty rounds down it as he drew level with it, hosing the carbine back and forth at waist level. He really couldn't afford the ammo, he had only one more magazine, but the side corridor was dark and he didn't want any nasty surprises.

He got one anyhow.

The automatic fire should have chopped any of the aliens standing between the knees and hips; probably it did. But one of them must have been hanging on the ceiling or stretched out on the floor. As soon as the burst of fire ended, the thing jumped out.

Bueller wasn't taking anything for granted, so he still had his weapon held ready, but the thing leapt as he fired again, flew like a missile at him.

Bueller's reactions were fast. It wouldn't matter how many rounds hit the damned thing, inertia would keep it coming. Bueller didn't have time to think. He dropped, slammed flat onto the slimy, hot floor, and the alien missed him by centimeters.

Mbutu yelled as the thing barreled into her. Blake fired, but the monster and Mbutu were entwined, and as good as Blake was, she couldn't stop the acid flow her shot caused. The spewing wound drenched Mbutu's face. She instinctively opened her mouth to scream. The thing was dying but it pumped enough of the corrosive blood onto Mbutu so she would join it shortly. Maybe she might have survived were she in a full-ride military medicator, but she'd never make it that far. Her cheeks and nose were a smoking ruin, her throat and lungs already being eaten away.

She would drown in her own fluids.

Bueller scrambled up. Mbutu made a strangled noise halfway between a moan and a plea. He knew what she wanted. He couldn't ask Blake to do it. Bueller pointed his carbine, tapped the trigger once.

The bullet in her brain ended Mbutu's suffering.

Blake nodded. "Thanks," she said.

Bueller had trouble drawing enough air to breathe. He shuddered.

Two of them left.

"There it is," Wilks said.

The front view screens gave a better picture than the ports, but Billie stared through the clear shields, preferring the reality. The mound sprawled upon the ground like a malignant tumor, dull gray in the light of the local sun. It was a desolate landscape, cleared around the hive of everything but dust and rock.

"I'm going to put down on that little ridge," Wilks said. "We can use the ship's guns better on the high ground and we'll be able to see them coming. And anything that might be chasing them."

She looked at him.

"Still too much interference," he said. "Something in the walls is blocking the com's signal."

"I could go—" Billie began.

"No. You can't."

"Man, oh, man," Blake said, "I'm definitely crossing this place *off* my vacation list. It stinks in here."

The winding corridor had provided them with more attackers, but it was wide enough that the red eyes let them see in time. Bueller and Blake took the aliens out as soon as they spotted them, and it had almost gotten to the point of target shooting for Bueller. He'd switched to semiauto to conserve ammo. He had about eighty rounds left, but also had Mbutu's plasma rifle slung over his shoulder. Things could be worse.

A large archway loomed.

"Signal is coming from in there," Blake said. "Less than fifty meters."

"The hatching room," Bueller said.

"Yeah."

"Let's do it."

The heat intensified as they neared the archway, the air thickened even more with stench and high humidity. It felt like the inside of a steambath full of rotting corpses.

Bueller darted through the opening, Blake backing in behind him, her rifle pointed to the rear.

"There they are," he said.

Four people, three men and a woman, webbed to the walls in that gauzy, spidery goo the things used.

The garbage-can-sized eggs sat impassively on the floor. There was no sign of the queen, no other drones around. It was quiet enough so Bueller could hear his own breathing.

The two of them moved quickly.

"This one is dead," Blake said, her fingers on the carotid of one of the women.

"This one, too," Bueller said.

One of them was alive, though. The marines tore away the sticky webbing. The eggs next to the man were still closed, he hadn't been implanted yet.

He came to as they were dragging him free of the web. He screamed.

"Easy, easy!" Blake said. "It's okay, we got you!"

Fear had stolen his words. The man tried to speak, stammered, gave up.

"Can you walk?"

He nodded, still mute.

"Then let's make tracks, fast, understand?"

He nodded again.

The three of them started for the chamber's exit. When they reached it, Bueller stopped.

Blake raised an eyebrow at him. "What?"

"I'll just leave them a couple of grenades for a going away present," he said. He hip-pointed his carbine and launched three rounds, fast, so the first explosion was still expanding as the second and third rounds flew. The sound was deafening, despite the spike muters the marines wore.

"Go, go!"

They ran.

* * *

Wilks touched a control on the sensor board. "Got seismic activity in there. Looks like somebody fired some explosive armament. M-40s, probably."

"They're still alive," Billie said.

"Maybe."

"We have to *do* something!"

"We *are* doing something. We're waiting. Won't help anybody if we don't have a way off this damned rock. In five hours the whole planet is going to get hammered flat as the oceans on Jupiter. We don't want to be here then."

"To your left!" Bueller yelled.

Blake, cool as liquid oxygen, turned and painted the corridor green with her plasma. The withering beams cooked the onrushing alien drones like crabs under their shells. Fluid boiled from their joints in deadly steam, but far enough away so there was no danger to the marines or the crewman.

"Eat hot plasma death, alien scum," Blake said.

Bueller stared at her.

"I always wanted to say that," she said. She smiled.

He shook his head. But he shared her feeling; against all the odds, they were nearing the exit to this nightmare. Less than a hundred meters away the harsh daylight of the planet spilled into the mound, giving them a light at the end of a very dangerous tunnel.

"Almost there," Bueller said. "Can you make it?"

The crewman finally found his voice. "I'll make it. Just keep those bastards off us."

The last thirty meters were the worst. It was clear,

no drones in front of them, but the run for the way out filled Bueller with hope—they might really make it after all—and it was too soon for that kind of optimism.

Still, they reached the mouth of the tunnel.

"Hel-*lo*, sunshine!" Blake said as they stepped out of the mound. Bueller had the tail, he kept his weapon and his gaze behind them, but the pressure of the light on his bare skin felt as good as anything ever had.

Blake said, "Sonofa*bitch*, our ride is here! There's the APC!"

Bueller spared a glance. Yes. There it was, on a slight ridge five hundred meters away.

Blake laughed. "Let's go home, folks!"

Bueller managed a chuckle. There was something wonderful about the air, bad as it was. And aside from Billie, he'd never seen anything quite as beautiful as that combat-camoed drop ship perched almost within spitting distance. "I hear that," he said. "Move out, I'll cover our asses."

Blake led the crewman down the incline from the mound along the dusty trail.

"There they are," Wilks said, his voice quiet and edgy.

Billie jerked around. Too far away to tell by direct visual who they were. Three of them. Two moving down the slope to the mound's entrance, one standing guard behind them.

Billie reached for the view enhancer, tapped the magnification up, looked at the screen.

The one in the entrance was Mitch.

Alive!

"Only three of them left," Wilks said. "Two marines and one crewman."

Billie didn't care. One of them was Mitch, he was okay, that was all that mattered.

"1st squad, this is Wilks. You copy?"

A woman's voice came back. "Glad you could drop by, Sarge. But I think the party's over. What say we pack it in and junk this place?"

"Yeah," Wilks said. "Hurry up, Blake, the meter is running."

"On our way."

Mitch heard the com and grinned. He stared into the darkness of the mound's gaping mouth. He started backing away, weapon still trained on the entrance. "Hey, Billie," he said into his com. "Hope you kept it warm for me."

"Come and get it," Billie said.

He half turned to look at the APC, the smile bright and happy.

A mistake.

The alien must have been waiting in the darkness for some break in Bueller's attention. It came clattering out, claws scraping and digging into the rocky surface as it cleared the entrance, arms extended, teeth revealed in a moray eel's needle grin.

Bueller twisted, swung the carbine around. Slipped on a loose piece of rock. Shifted, off balance, to his left. The carbine's barrel dropped, just a hair, as he fired.

Fired, and missed.

He tried to correct his aim, the thing was almost

on top of him and he only needed to pointshoot, but he was too slow. It crossed its hands, grabbed him, digging one steel-hard claw into his ribs, the other on the opposite side, just under his hip. Talons bit deep. The carbine flew from Bueller's grip. He tried to draw the slug pistol.

"Mitch!" Billie screamed from his com.

The alien flexed muscles hidden under its exoskeleton, cords filled with power a score of times stronger than a man could manage. Bueller felt the pain burn through his waist, a shattering bolt that short-circuited all his systems, filling him, like a sudden plunge into molten aluminum. He managed a scream, then felt the unendurable shock as—

As the thing tore him in half at the waist.

Billie saw the parts of Bueller fall. Saw his hips and legs fly one way, his upper body another. Tumbling, and the white circulating fluid—not red blood, white, *white!*—spraying like a milky fountain into the air under the alien sun.

24

Wilks watched the alien rip Bueller apart.

He yelled into the com. "Blake, get down!" He slapped the fire controls for the robot guns trained on the mouth of the alien hive. He saw the edges of the entrance light with tiny flashes as the 20mm expended uranium slugs chattered against the walls inside. Having a specific target, the robot gun hosed it in bursts of twenty, S-shaped patterns from top to bottom, stopping a meter or so short of the ground.

The gunfire chopped the alien into pieces, blowing the shattered parts back against the hive like a swat from a giant steel broom. The fire computer locked in the shape of the alien and shut the gun down, waiting for more targets that looked like him.

Billie screamed. She was looking at the viewer

and it was dialed up so she couldn't miss what Bueller was. The ancillary nodes of his digestive system hung from his torso; white polymer circulating fluid oozed over everything. Where a human would be soaked with blood and painted bright crimson, Bueller was drenched in milky froth. Tubules, shunts, circulatory lines, all splayed from the ruined android body.

Billie screamed again, a wordless cry. Wilks knew then she'd never suspected.

"Billie!"

She kept yelling.

He didn't have time for this. Over her din, he yelled into the com. "Blake! Move it! Stay low, you're clear to one meter only!"

The computer triggered the robot gun again. Wilks only saw the aliens for a second before the things were punched back into the mound.

Blake moved, but the wrong way. She crawled back to where Bueller lay, staying under the gun's field of fire.

"Blake, goddammit!"

Billie screamed again.

Wilks slid the control chair over a meter, reached out, slapped Billie's face. Her scream stopped as if cut off by a laser harvester.

"He's alive," Blake said over the com. She hoisted the terribly wounded android onto her back and crawled back to where the crewman lay.

"Oh, God, oh, God, oh, God," Billie said.

Wilks lost it. "I tried to fucking warn you! I tried to keep you away from him! You wouldn't listen to me! Yes, he's an android. The whole platoon, all of them, they're *all* androids! Created for a mission like this. How do you think they managed to breathe that thin air and keep going?"

Billie stared at the screen, not blinking, not moving.

Blake zigzagged, cleared the APC's gun line, and stood, Bueller still on her back. Half of Bueller. The crewman was right behind her.

"That's why they had to go back into the mound," Wilks said, feeling very tired all of a sudden. "They couldn't let the humans die. It's the First Law."

Billie stared straight ahead.

"They're faster, stronger, cheaper than we are to maintain. Some people didn't like working with them, so the new experimental models were made to pass for human. They eat, drink, piss, act, and even feel like humans. They can hate, fear, love, just like we do. From the outside, even an expert can't tell. Everything external looks just the same. But I guess you know that, don't you?"

Finally she turned to look at him. He could see her pain, it went all the way to her core. She had fallen in love with an android, had slept with him. For some people, that would be the same as falling in love with a dog or a farm animal and having sex with it.

"The pirates didn't know," he continued. "That's why the aliens weren't in any hurry to attack the marines and use them for incubators. Their flesh wouldn't support the babies. They look the same, feel the same to the touch, but apparently they don't *taste* very good.

"I'm sorry, kid."

When she spoke, her voice was as cold as deep space. "Why didn't you tell me, Wilks?"

"I tried. You didn't want to hear it."

"You never said anything about androids."

"By the time I realized I should, it was too late. What was I supposed to say? You're in love with an artificial person? He was born in a vat and put together like a puzzle by a bunch of androtechs? You wouldn't have believed it."

"You should have told me."

"Yeah, well, my life is full of things I should have done and didn't. This mission is screwed, and we're leaving. The rest of it we sort out later."

Billie turned back to the screen. Blake and the crewman had what was left of Bueller cradled between them and were approaching the APC at a quick jog. Behind them the mouth of the aliens' nest erupted with dozens of the things. The robot gun worked its deadly magic, hammering the creatures with chunks of armor-piercing death, battering them to pieces; still, they boiled forth like angry fire ants, ran into the wall of metal, and shattered against it. Dozens, scores, hundreds of them—they kept coming.

The robot gun was state of the art, it locked on to the acquired targets, calculated for local gravity, windage, movement, then fired efficiently and dispatched them. But no matter how efficient a weapon, it could only live as long as it was fed.

The last of the ammunition ran through the electronic machinery. The control panel lit with a flashing red light. The gun, said the computer, was empty. Since further identified-by-image targets

were in evidence, the computer hereby advised the
primary operator that reloading was now required
for continued operation. Since the spare ammunition module had already been expended, the primary operator was hereby notified that additional
modules would have to be manually inserted for
continued operation. Meanwhile, the system would
remain on standby, identifying and tracking i-b-i
targets.

Wilks shook his head. Bad news. The APC had
shot up all the ammunition it carried. Nobody had
figured a lot of air-to-air combat would be happening on this mission. And the aliens kept bounding
out of that damned nest like giant black termites
stoked on steroids and amphetamines. Must be fifty
of them heading toward the ship, despite all the
ones the gun had blown away. More of the things
climbed over the piled bodies as he watched. Time
to leave.

Blake and the crewman and Bueller were only
fifty meters away from the ship. Wilks ordered the
outer hatch open.

"Triple time, marine," he said to Blake. "There's
a shitload of company behind you coming up fast
and I want to shut the door real soon now!"

They were close enough so Wilks could see their
expressions now. The crewman turned and looked
over his shoulder, and apparently didn't like what
he saw. He was the limiting factor, Blake could run
probably twice his best, even carrying Bueller. The
crewman speeded up, and Blake matched him.

For no reason he could think of, Wilks was reminded of an old joke, one that he'd heard as a kid,

about sheep herders. Come on guys. What say, let's
get the flock out of here. . . .

Billie was numb, all the way to her soul. Wilks
had slapped her, but she couldn't feel anything but
a little heat where his palm had struck.

Lies. It was all lies. Everything. How could Mitch
have done it? Why hadn't he told her the truth?

Bootsteps clattered up the entry ramp. They were
here.

Blake entered the cabin. She squatted and carefully eased Mitch onto the deck. There was an aid
kit on the wall, but Blake passed it and pulled a
plastic box from a cabinet instead. Of course. A
human aid kit wouldn't help.

The crewman said, "Go, man, get us the hell out
of here!"

Wilks was in the pilot's seat. "Strap in," he ordered.

Only the crewman hustled to obey. Billie stood
over Mitch. His eyes were closed. He ended at the
waist and what spilled from his torso was ugly to
look upon.

"Sit down, Billie!"

She still didn't move.

Mitch opened his eyes. For a moment they were
unfocused, but then she saw him recognize her.
"I—I'm s-s-sorry, B-Billie," he said. His voice bubbled, as if he were talking underwater. "I—I w-was
going to t-t-tell you." He gasped, trying to get more
air to work his voice.

Blake had the box open. She pulled several small
electronic devices out and slapped them against

Mitch's shoulder and chest. Another one on his neck, yet another to his temple. She ran a tube from a plastic bag of clear fluid into the device on his neck. The liquid began to flow through the tubing. Blake pulled a plastic can out and sprayed a bluish foam all over the torn waist. The foam crackled and bubbled and quickly settled into a thick film that changed from blue to a bright green, coating all the exposed nodules and tubing.

"Is he going to die?" Billie asked.

"I don't know," Blake said. "His system valves have shut down all the torn circulators and the self-repair programs are running. It's a lot of damage, but we're designed to withstand a lot."

"Sit the fuck down!" Wilks roared. "We've got to lift, now!"

Billie moved to a seat, still watching Blake work on Mitch. Blake hooked one hand under a stanchion, the other she put against Mitch's chest. "I'm anchored," she said. "And I've got him held stable. Go."

Wilks cycled the hatch closed and initiated the lift program. The ship's repellors cycled up, whining as they came on line. "Sequencing for lift off," he said. "Stand by—"

Something slammed into the APC, hard enough to jolt the vessel, to make it ring with the impact.

"Shit!" the crewman said.

More impacts. Three. Five. Ten of them.

"They are all over us!" the crewman yelled.

"Fuck 'em," Wilks said. "We're gone." He punched a control.

Nothing happened.

"What the hell?" the crewman began.

"One of them is blocking a thrust skirt tube," Wilks said. "The computer won't fire it. I'll have to go to manual—"

There came a screech as metal tore.

"They're digging through the hull," Billie said.

"That's impossible!" the crewman said.

Another *grinch!* of metal being clawed by something harder than it was.

Wilks tapped controls. The APC shook, but lifted, wobbled a little, but rose slowly. Went up a couple hundred meters, Billie could see through the forward screens.

"All right!" the crewman yelled.

"We're too heavy," Wilks said. "We'll have to shake the fuckers off—"

The ship lurched, dropped, twisting to port as though a heavy weight had landed on that side. A siren began screaming from the control panel. Wilks worked frantically, hands dancing rapidly back and forth. The APC began to level but it continued to settle. "That's the left repellor," Wilks said. "Emergency brake-lock. Something is inside the housing. I can't override."

"But—but the housing is armored!" the crewman said.

"The intake is protected by a finger-thick wire mesh," Wilks said. "But something went through it. The computer knows the danger. The carbon-boron blades are supercooled, they're brittle. They hit something bigger than a few grams, they'll shatter and blow us to pieces. I can't compensate enough with the other repellors to get us into orbit. We'll have to land and clear the housing."

"You mean go *outside*?"

Wilks stared at the crewman. "Unless you got a better idea."

"Oh, man!"

Thumping continued on the hull, more squeals as the metal bent or gave up the fight.

Billie stared at Mitch. He looked at her, his eyes clear. She didn't know what to say. She'd lain naked with this man—no, not a man, an *android*—had shared her body with him, had told him her secrets. Had given him her truth, for whatever it was worth. And he had responded as a man, but he had also kept from her the biggest truth of all.

As she watched him lay there, possibly dying, she felt outraged, felt sick, felt that if she never saw him again it would be too soon. And yet.

And yet, another feeling stirred deep inside her mind, at the threshold of her perceptions. It was a feeling she could not deny, despite what he had done. She didn't want to look at the thing looming there, didn't want to know about it, didn't want to acknowledge it. She tried to close the door between her and that stirring, to make it go away, but looking at him, she couldn't.

Well. It didn't matter. They were all going to die here. It wouldn't be long before the aliens clawed their way in. Billie looked at the weapons Blake still carried. Wilks wouldn't let the things take them alive. It would be quick, if it came to that. So it didn't matter what she was feeling about Mitch. No. Nothing mattered. Her short and mostly unhappy time was about to come to its end. Except for the few hours when she'd thought Mitch was other than he turned out to be, it hadn't been much of a life. Maybe she should tell him that, since they were going to die.

Or maybe not. What difference did it make?

The APC reached the ground, settled unevenly.

"Maybe we crushed a couple of them underneath," Wilks said.

Billie stared at him. That didn't matter either.

They were all going to die. The way she felt at the moment, it would be a relief.

25

The thumps against the hull increased. The external pickups were mostly blocked by the alien forms as they mindlessly beat against the ship, as if it were alive and they were trying to kill it.

Wilks looked at the others. Billie was sunk into a stunned silence. The crewman was so frightened he had wet himself. Bueller drifted in and out of consciousness. Blake was the only one he could depend on for help; she was the one to guard his back while he went outside to clear the grid.

Wilks smiled wryly. Right. Opening the hatch would be fun. They didn't have enough firepower in the APC to keep the things off him long enough to do what had to be done. He'd been too rattled to think earlier. The reasonable thing was to get the ship into the air again, move it ten or fifteen klicks away from the nest, and deal with the few aliens that hung on to them once they landed.

Except that they didn't have much fuel to play around with here, and a miscalculation would leave them shy of what they needed to reach the ship in orbit. He had locked the *Benedict*'s comp into the nuclear scenario; it wasn't going to be altered from the APC, couldn't be. He'd wanted to be sure, in case something happened to them.

Well, looked like worst had come to worst.

"Sarge?"

He looked at Blake. "No, going outside isn't real swift. I'm going to take it up again, do a roll, and move us far enough away so we can put down without company."

Blake nodded. "Makes sense."

"If we're light on fuel after that, we'll gut this sucker and toss out everything that adds unnecessary weight."

Wilks worked the controls. The ship trembled, but didn't go anywhere.

"Oh, shit!" he said.

"Sarge?"

"Either too many of 'em on us or they've jammed up the other grids. Looks like we're back to plan A."

Metal screeched.

"Damn."

"I wouldn't want to bet on us pulling this off, Sarge."

"Yeah, me neither. I don't see as how we have any choice. Listen, Blake, if they get me alive, you punch my lights out, you copy?"

"I can't, Sarge, you know that."

"Oh, yeah, right. Never mind. I got Massey's grenade here. I'll pull my own plug, it comes to that."

"Billie."

She looked at him, her eyes dull. "What?"

"Take this pistol. If we don't come back . . ."

She nodded, understanding.

The ship rocked. Raised up on the starboard side, fell back.

"Uh-oh," Wilks said. "They're working together. Enough of them will tip us over. Get to the hatch, Blake."

She nodded. Unslung her plasma rifle and switched off the safety.

The ship rocked again. Slammed back into place.

"Billie. Look, I'm sorry for getting you into this."

"It's okay, Wilks. I didn't have anything better to do."

For a second their gazes locked and they smiled at each other. The borrowed time they'd both been living on was about to expire.

Fuck it, Wilks thought. He took a deep breath. "Let's do it—"

The ship *thrummed,* a sound unlike anything Wilks had ever heard washed over them, vibrating every surface in the APC, battering at his ears like padded pugil sticks. He dropped to his knees and clapped his hands over his ears. He felt the vibration to his core; it made the marrow in his bones hum.

"Chreesto!" the crewman screamed.

Abruptly the sound died.

Wilks stood, shaken. What the hell had that been?

"Listen," Blake said.

"I don't hear anything," the crewman said.

Wilks nodded. "That's right. The aliens have stopped attacking us."

It was as quiet as an isolation chamber.

They all looked at Wilks.

"Let's take a look, Blake."

Wilks took a couple of deep breaths, then moved to the hatch. He held the carbine ready, Blake with her rifle right behind him. The hatch went up.

"Oh, man," Blake said.

Wilks was speechless. At least fifty of the aliens lay sprawled on the ground around the ship. They looked . . . melted, as if all their edges had run together. Dead, Wilks didn't doubt it for a second. That was pretty incredible. But what he saw standing a dozen meters away was even more incredible.

"What the hell is that?" Blake said.

Wilks just stared.

Some kind of suited figure stood there. It was easily seven or eight meters tall, bipedal, with a clear helmet on the E-suit it wore. Wilks could see the thing's face behind the bubble covering, and it looked like nothing so much as an elephant might appear, were it to evolve to a two-legged animal. It had pinkish-gray skin, a ridged nose or maybe a trunk that vanished in a long chamber down the front of the suit, with what seemed to be a pair of small tentacles, one to either side of the larger trunk. It had a short extension of the suit behind it, and Wilks guessed that it had a tail in the tube, shaped like a skinny pyramid. A closer look and Wilks realized the thing wasn't exactly standing.

The heavy boots it wore had a central split, as if the thing had hooves, and they didn't quite touch the ground. It was actually *floating* a couple of centimeters above the surface.

It was close enough so he could see its eyes. The pupils were shaped like crosses, wider than they were high. They looked dead, those eyes.

The thing held a device in its gauntleted hands and Wilks would bet ten years pay against a toenail clipping it was some kind of weapon.

The air was thin and Wilks had to take big gulps of it to get enough oxygen. He glanced over and saw that Blake was slowly bringing her rifle around to bear on the thing.

"Negative on that," he said softly. "I think this thing just flattened all the local bad guys with whatever that gear is it's holding. I don't want it to think we mean it any harm. If it can knock down that many of those suckers all at once, we're way outgunned here."

Blake let her rifle droop, to point at the ground.

The thing—another alien, and sure as shit not from around here, Wilks knew—pointed its own weapon downward.

"Hello, spacer," Blake said softly. "You must be new in town."

Behind them, Billie screamed in terror.

Billie was back on Rim.

She was a child, sitting in the front of her father's scout hopper, watching the near featureless gray pass by the observation port. So far the ride had been dull, but her father had said there was something out there they had to go look at and he brought her and her brother Vick along. Her father's assistant, Mr. Zendall, was also there. Her father called him Gene, but she wasn't supposed to call him that. And her mother was there, too.

"Holy Sister of the Stars," her father said.

"Russ? What is it?" her mother said.

"Our detectors just went off the scale. There's something huge down there, in the Valley of the Iron Fingers."

"How can that be?"

"I don't know. But we're talking about megaton-nage, a mixed signal. Got to be man-made. Gene?"

"I got it, Russ. Lord, Lord. I can't get a configuration ID on it. Look at the specs."

It didn't mean anything to Billie, all the numbers and stuff, but she knew it must be important because her parents and Gene—Mr. Zendall—were all excited.

"It's shaped like a giant horseshoe."

Billie didn't know what that meant, she'd never seen a horse except in edcom and that one hadn't been wearing any shoes she could see.

"Gene, Sarah, I think we've got an alien ship here."

They landed, and even through the swirling murk Billie could see what had her parents so excited. It was like a big U, the ends pointing up at an angle. It was real big, you could put a lot of scout hoppers in it and have room left over.

"No match to anything on record," Gene said. He laughed.

"How could colony tracking have missed it?" her mother said.

"Magnetic interference from the iron, maybe," her father said. "And the weathersats probably don't footprint this spot. Who cares? We found it, we've got salvage rights on it. This might be our ticket back to Earth. It could be worth a fortune!"

They landed the hopper. Her father and mother and Gene put on E-suits. "You stay here and watch us on the monitor," her father said. "Don't let Vick touch any of the controls. We're going to go look at the ship. If you get hungry, there are ration packs in the storebox. One each, no more, okay?"

Billie nodded. "Okay."

So then she watched. All three of them had cams on their suits and she knew how to switch around so she could see from one or the other or all three at once, if she wanted to.

At first it was dark, outside was stormy like usual, but pretty soon they got into the big ship and it got better. They had floodlights and turned them on.

The inside was spooky, weird, it didn't look like anything Billie had ever seen. It took her parents and Gene a long time to get to the control room—she knew that was where they wanted to go because she could hear them talking on their suit coms.

And when they finally got there—Billie had gone to the toilet twice and already eaten her meal pack and half of Vick's because he didn't like the green paste and she did—there was a dead thing sitting in the control seat.

It was real big, and it looked strange. Kind of like the edcom of a big terran animal called an elephant.

It had a big, funny nose and overall its whole body was as long as four men, but it was dead, lying on its back. There was a hole in its stomach or its chest or something, with bones sticking up from the hole. Yuk.

Her parents went around the thing a few times, talking to each other and to Gene. And then they went down the hall. To a big room. And on the floor of the big room were these things. . . .

Billie screamed, and Wilks was there, holding her by the shoulders, shaking her gently.

"Hey, hey, it's all right. We're okay."

The memories bubbled in her, and she fought them. But there was a pressure in her brain, a kind of malevolent presence.

"Billie?"

"It's that thing out there," she said. "I can read its thoughts. More like its feelings. It's inside my head."

Wilks glanced at Blake.

"I'm not crazy," Billie said. "It just killed all the aliens outside our ship, right? Because it hates them. It—its kind—have been here before. Collecting specimens. I, oh, God!"

"Billie!"

She shook her head, as if that would clear the intrusion by the stranger. "It somehow can feel my thoughts, too," she said. "It knows."

"Knows what?"

"I—on Rim—my parents . . ."

"What about them?"

"Oh, God, Wilks! My parents found a ship there.

An alien ship. The pilot was some kind of scientist, maybe. It had been to this world. It had taken specimens of these things. Eggs. It must have been infected, implanted. They killed it. The ship crashed on Rim. The things survived inside it, I don't know for how long. My—my parents found it. They went into the ship. . . ."

Wilks hugged her. "Easy, kid. Let it go. We know what happened."

Billie sobbed. Tears flowed. That was one of the memories she had buried the deepest. Not even the worst of her nightmares had dredged it up before now.

Hate filled her brain, but it was not her own emotion. It was from the space traveler floating outside the APC, the giant whose fellow being had died and crashed into Rim.

She didn't want to remember, but the space traveler pulled at it, drawing it into view. The child she had been, watching the monitors. Watching her father lean over one of the eggs. Seeing all over again the opening and the crablike embryo that flew out and latched on to her father's face. Seeing her mother and Gene drag him out. Listening to the screams . . .

"No! Get out of me! Go away!"

Hate. Gut-churning, black, molten hate, sloshing over and filling Billie to her toes. How this thing hated these creatures!

"It saved us," Wilks said.

"Not because it likes us," she said. "Because it can't stand them."

Blake said, "Sarge, we've got to get the ship spaceworthy. We've got what? three hours?"

Billie thought about the bombs that would drop, what would happen to the planet when they did.

She felt a sudden interest from the spacesuited figure. It understood her thoughts well enough to hear that message.

"The thing is leaving," the crewman said. "Just floating away."

"It knows about the bombs," Billie said.

"Yeah, well, while I'd like to be an ambassador to a new species and all, we have to get the APC fixed or we're going to be atomic dust ourselves."

Wilks stood, leaving Billie sitting on the deck of the little craft. Next to her, Mitch opened his eyes. He didn't speak, and Billie had nothing she wanted to say to him. The alien presence left her suddenly, a sharp sensation as if a knife were pulled from her brain.

It was hard to breathe, their eyes burned and their noses ached and dripped, but the repairs took only an hour.

The APC lifted, made orbit, and managed a safe rendezvous with the *Benedict*. Wilks made very certain there were no unwanted passengers on the APC before he pulled into the bay, and even then, he had the cleaning lasers scorch every bit of the landing craft's exterior before he let them leave the docking area.

Blake plugged Bueller into some kind of life-support system designed for androids.

The crewman—Billie didn't know his name and

didn't care if she ever did—went to do checks on the ship.

Wilks went to do something, he didn't say what.

Billie sat at a table, staring at the wall. It was over. They had come to the aliens' world. They had survived pirates and attacks by the creatures; they were about to smash the planet back to a pre-life stage. They were going home.

It was all over.

And she didn't give a damn.

26

Orona sat in his office, watching the three corporation executives seated across from him. The doctor was named Dryner; he couldn't remember the others' names, but thought of them by the clothing they wore: Red and Green.

The room walls were shielded, even the windows were lined with breakup softwires so a laser listener couldn't pick up conversations from outside. Orona suspected that at least one of the three corporation men carried some kind of scrambler to block electronic eavesdropping, maybe they all did. They'd been scanned, but there were some remarkable plastics around these days that could mimic just about anything. A shoe, a kneecap, whatever. Conversations held at this high a level were best done with great care. Nobody would be collecting Orona's words, either.

"All right, gentlemen, let's not do an elaborate mating dance all around it. We all know why we're here."

Green and Red exchanged quick, shielded glances, no expressions to read. They'd be good poker players, Orona figured. The medical VP was also cool, but a bit more nervous. He tapped a finger lightly against his thigh.

"Perhaps we should reconsider having attorneys present," Red said.

"Nobody is talking about prosecution," Orona said. "Let's not insult each other's intelligence. I'm government and you're private, my hammer is bigger, and I'd play hell whacking you with it, we all know that, too. At least right now, anyway."

Red and Green smiled, identical expressions. They knew that.

"So let's skip the scat and get to the bottom line," Orona said. "You had one of the aliens tucked away down in your SA lab and some religious fanatics broke in and got themselves impregnated by the thing's embryos. We all know that.

"Your specimen got cooked in the explosion that destroyed the lab. The fanatics got away. We know that because we are still getting reports of the nightmares, so some of the damned things are still alive.

"Am I telling you anything you don't know?"

Red and Green smiled slightly, as one. Men of the world had certain sources. No point in denying it.

The doctor, Dryner, shook his head. "We, ah, are aware of this."

"I thought you might be. Got a tap in our main-frame. But you don't have a line tied to our Tac Unit."

He looked at them. Red shrugged, the barest hint of a moment. Orona read that as a "no."

"Well, we've found one of the attackers."

The doctor leaned forward, eager. "With the implanted embryo?"

"Unfortunately, no. This man's chest had been burst from the inside. He'd been dead for half a day when our team uncovered him in New Chicago. There was no sign of the newborn alien."

The doctor leaned back. "Shit," he said. His voice was soft.

"I share your sentiments, Doctor. We would very much like to collect these things ourselves. But I'm afraid our worry is now larger than simply who'll be the first to get a potential weapons system, no matter how valuable that might be."

Green and Red perked up. Green said, "What do you mean?"

Orona stood, turned to look through the window at the city lights kicking on as darkness gathered in the dusk. Traffic zipped back and forth in the airlanes, glittering in the final rays of the setting sun. "Doctor, you understand how these things reproduce. Each one is a potential queen, is it not?"

Dryner looked at the other two company men. They gave him those tiny shrugs. Go ahead.

The doctor said, "Yes, that is possible."

"We don't know how many of the fanatics escaped. Could be as many as a dozen. We've lost one of the newborn aliens. The others will all be hatching from their human 'eggs' shortly, if they haven't already done so, is that not correct?"

"Well, it would depend on which eggs delivered their implants. The queen laid them over several days."

"But at the most, several days plus or minus is all, correct?"

"I'm afraid so."

"Doctor, if there were, oh, say, five of them implanted, and each of them produces a queen and they all begin to lay eggs as soon as they reach maturity, how long do you think it might take before the damned things are swarming all over the place?"

Dryner swallowed dryly. "I—there's no way to be certain, that is to say—"

Orona turned around. Felt the weight of the entire government on his shoulders. He was the expert, though these men might know as much as he did. He needed every scrap of knowledge he could get. "It's rather like the hamster problem. If one mother and her litters all come to term and keep mating and having more babies who all survive, in a couple of years we're knee-deep in hamsters.

"Of course, that doesn't happen. Some are killed by the mothers, some are eaten by natural predators, some get stepped on by things with big feet. But these aliens don't *have* any natural predators on this world.

"It takes armor-piercing military-grade weaponry to kill one and even then it isn't easy. We have the reports from our Colonial Marines' encounters with them. A Chinese farmer with a pitchfork, an Australian bird hunter with a shotgun, they'll be wasting their time trying to stop a full-grown alien with either of those weapons, correct?"

The doctor swallowed again. The question was rhetorical.

"In fact, just about anybody who comes against one of these things is going to regret it. They reproduce like hamsters, the queens don't even need mates, they come of age real fast. We don't know where they will start to pop up. The fanatics have spread out, we've gotten reports of them all over the globe. Some have to be discounted, of course, but if a tenth of the material is correct, we are going to start seeing these things making themselves known in both hemispheres from the equator to the poles. Chicago is a long way from Lima.

"And, gentlemen, that means we will all be in very deep shit. I expect your cooperation in every way to stop that. Because if we don't stop it, making that big end of the year bonus is going to be the last thing you have to worry about. These things will be killing so many people that you'll hear the survivors' outraged screams on Mars. And every one of them will be calling for heads to roll. I'll give them yours. Then the government will give them mine."

The doctor licked dry lips.

Even those two cosmopolitan men of the world, Red and Green, looked unhappy with that idea.

Good. Orona had them. Now, he hoped it wasn't too late. He didn't express his own worst fear: that the things would get well established enough so the very survival of mankind on the planet would be in jeopardy. Of course, that was worst-case scenario, he didn't really think that would happen, it was just a nightmarish worry.

He hoped.

27

The giant elephantlike creature had gotten away, they saw the ion trail of its ship dispersing in the vacuum before they broke their own vessel out of its ellipse around the aliens' world. Funny, the place didn't even have a name, at least not one Wilks knew about. Not that he worried about it.

There wasn't anything down there to worry about.

So. The hard rain began to fall upon the aliens' planet, courtesy of the Colonial Marines and delivered by Sergeant Wilks. The chain-link nukes seeded from the *Benedict* dropped from their computer-designed orbits and drizzled across the harsh land; some fell into the sea, though the water harmed them not in the least.

When the nukes chained and went off, they

smashed at the planet as might a raging god grown angry with his creation.

Sheets of atomic fire scoured the surface. Shock waves pounded trees and bushes and even some mountains flat. Volcanoes long dormant were shaken to life by the explosions, adding their blasts and lava spews to the chaos. The land groaned and responded with earthquakes that shook the surface harder than any man-made scale could register. Oceans boiled, steam rose; life in the sea, land, and air cooked where it swam or walked or flew. The world rattled to its very roots and whatever might have survived the initial devastation would fare poorly under the ensuing pall of the nuclear winter and radioactivity left by the deliberately dirty bombs. The aliens were hardy; they could survive in conditions that would kill most forms of life, but even they had to eat. Food was going to be scarce here for a long, long time.

Wilks watched on the monitors, the cams shielded by filters, as the aliens' planet spasmed and died. And he felt real good about it, too. He hoped they all lived long enough to starve. Slowly.

He didn't think he would be bothered much anymore by the nightmares he had lived with for so many years. He had struck back against the hellish things, and his punch had been a lot bigger than any they could throw. He had destroyed them. The last laugh was his.

Yeah, there was the one left on Earth, but when he got back, he was going to see what he could do about that one, too.

He wondered what the penalty for blowing up a

whole planet was? Why, he might be court-mar-tialed.

Imagine that.

It was worse than Orona had figured.

The first infestations seemed easy enough to deal with. His Tac teams were primed for sudden mass disappearances, and whenever an area starting missing people, they went in. He mobilized trans-portation so that a fully equipped team could launch and parabola down to any spot on the globe in under three hours.

The first nests were small, no more than fifty or a hundred eggs and a single queen. The Tac teams took no chances. They sterilized the area. The nests were razed, surrounding areas destroyed, suspected carriers picked up and detained. Those with im-plants were killed quickly and their bodies burned.

New Chicago, Lesser Miami, Havana, Madrid—those nests were quickly discovered and eliminated.

At first, Orona felt a certain smugness. True, there would be a lot of damages to cover and a certain amount of political heat to be endured, but the Planetary Security Act gave him a great deal of latitude. The things weren't very bright; they were like termites or ants or bees; they built their nests and set up egg chambers and sent workers out to gather food. The behavior was instinctive; there was no great intelligence behind it. It had apparently worked for the things on their homeworld, but there they didn't have such clever competition. For a time, Orona rested easier. He was the expert, and the military trusted him implicitly.

Weeks went by. Months.

More nests were kicked open: Paris, Moscow, Brisbane, Antarctic City. The things had spread far and wide as he had feared, but still they were easy enough to find and destroy. The infection was bad, but controlled. Like a staph boil lanced and cleaned, it would heal.

But then things began to change.

The Tac teams were getting good at their jobs, practice making them better, and maybe they started to get sloppy. Or maybe it was some kind of forced natural selection. Like rats or roaches who have been hunted and poisoned or smashed flat, the aliens began to vary their nest making.

The hives got smaller and more numerous. The Tac teams would find only ten or fifteen eggs in a tiny chamber, and such places were harder to locate. And there were more of them. An area of Greater North Africa in the old Ivory Coast yielded no less than eighty small nests inside a fifty-kilometer circle. Some of the hives were in Abidan, in the basements of skyscrapers or old warehouses, but some of them were in the surrounding countryside, under the ground. Tac squads discovered implanted cattle, horses, and even goats in some chambers. Anything large enough seemed to work. And while people in civilized countries who went missing were usually reported, a farmer and a few dozen cattle in some rural area might not be noticed.

It was as though the aliens were becoming smarter as a survival characteristic.

Six months after the escape from the labs in

Lima, Orona had to order a division-sized attack on a giant nest in Diego Suarez, on the northern tip of Madagascar. It was actually a series of several hundred smaller nests that had been tunneled and joined together.

Eight months into the war, Orona was responsible for the nuclear destruction of Jakarta.

A year after the war began, the continent of Australia was considered too infested to allow any travel to or from, and a full quarantine was instigated. Any ship, air vessel, or spacecraft trying to leave was shot down by Coast Guard laser satellites.

It was no longer a matter of Tac units seeking alien hives to destroy. It was a matter of establishing perimeters and checking to make certain no carriers crossed into safe territories. It was truly war.

Martial law was declared. All national boundaries were suspended. The Military Alliance came into being and civil liberties were put aside for the duration of the conflict. Suspected carriers of alien embryos could be legally shot by the command of any military officer above the rank of colonel. Then it dropped to majors and captains. Then sergeants. Pretty soon, any soldier with a gun could shoot anybody he damned well wanted to, and if the scan came up negative later, well, too fucking bad. War was hell, wasn't it? A few civilians here and there to save the planet? Yes.

Alien drones that were captured—a rare event—seemed to have gotten a little brighter. The smartest could barely keep up with an average dog, insofar as intelligence was concerned. But the single queen captured in a battle that destroyed half of San

Francisco's downtown district tested out to nearly 175 on the Irwin-Schlatler scale. That made it smarter than most of the humans ever born.

The nightmares had come true. Whatever Orona had felt before was nothing compared to the sinking, twisting coldness in his gut when *that* little bit of information arrived in his computer. They *were* getting smarter. Too smart.

And humans were responsible for it.

Onboard the *Benedict*, the survivors of the trip prepared for hypersleep.

Bueller lay in his rigged device, alive and stable, according to Blake. Billie had avoided him, but she couldn't get into her sleep chamber without a final confrontation. She had to speak to him.

He was shrouded in a hyperbaric sleeve from the chest down to where the rest of him had been. From there up, he looked as he had before. He was awake when she entered the room. They were alone.

"Mitch."

"Billie. I—I would rather you didn't see me like this."

"Well, that's too goddamned bad! How else would you have me see you? Like a man?"

"I'm sorry, Billie. You can't know how sorry."

"What was I, Mitch? A glitch in your programming?" She moved closer to him. She could have reached out and touched him. Could have. Would not.

"No," he said.

"Then what?"

"I should have told you. I tried, but I just couldn't. I was afraid."

"Afraid?"

"Of losing you."

She laughed, a short, sharp, bitter sound.

"I can't help what I am, Billie. I didn't have a choice in how I was born."

"Right, but you decided to fool the stupid human bitch, didn't you?"

"No. Whatever I am, wherever I came from, I eat, I feel, I hurt. And, I found out, I love."

Billie bit at her lip. She didn't want to hear this.

She wanted to hear it more than anything.

"I'm not like you," he continued. "I didn't have a mother and father, never grew as a child, never had a life before I was created for the Colonial Marines. But I grow, after a fashion. I learn. I became more than I was. And I experienced love. I don't know if it is the same as you feel. For me, it's a hollowness that only being around you fills, an ache when you are away, a fever that only you can cool. I feel lust for you, tenderness, I want to touch you, hold you. Even now, when I'm only half alive."

He stopped. Sobbed.

Oh, God. Don't let him cry, she thought. She couldn't bear that.

"And I deceived you," he said. "But when that thing grabbed me, when it tore me in two, that wasn't as painful as what I felt when I saw you look at me. Saw you look at me and hate me—" he stopped. Turned his face away.

And Billie realized that what she had felt was real, whatever Mitch was. That she had loved him as he had loved her, for what he described was what she had felt.

What she *still* felt.

"Mitch . . ."

"Go, Billie. Turn off the machines. Let me die."

Now she did reach out and touch him. His bare shoulder was warm, the skin alive, the muscles solid. He loved her, she was convinced of that. Whatever else he might be, that counted for a lot. Nobody had loved her since her parents.

"Mitch," she said.

He turned to look up at her.

She bent. Kissed him softly on the lips. Felt his pain, and felt it ebb as he realized what she was doing. His arms came up, encircled her.

"Oh, God, Billie!"

"Shhh. It's all right. It's all right. It doesn't matter."

And it didn't matter. Not at all.

It was war, and men were losing.

Orona marveled at this, that it should come to be this way. Man had the superior technology, it was man's world, man had the advantages. Except—

Except that the aliens had a stronger drive to live. They would sacrifice all for that, for the survival of the species. Only a few rare men were willing to do that. A mother would die to protect her children; a saint would walk into the fire for his fellow men or his god, but the instinct of self-preservation was too strong in most humans. The aliens didn't care. If a hundred drones had to die to save one egg, then they would. And did.

The things sprang up everywhere, in places where a rat would have trouble living, in spots where no one would have guessed they could spawn. Buried in the arctic ice floes, in deserts, in the tamed jungles, on barges, anywhere there was room for a nest. Nobody knew how many of the things there were, there were only guesses. The estimates ranged from hundreds of thousands to tens of millions. Private ships left Earth in droves, so many the military couldn't stop or even inspect them all. Most only fled as far as Luna or the Belt, some could reach the far planets of the system. A few wealthy souls banded together and bought private starships before the government clamped down and made such ownership illegal. Thousands ran, because on Earth, there were few places left to hide.

Orona was in one of those places, a heavily guarded military complex in Mexico. The perimeter was ringed with force fences, the ground mined, every car or air carrier that entered or left scanned, every passenger fluoroviewed for parasites. It was as safe as anywhere left.

In the end, Orona finally realized that the aliens were like a disease, not like an enemy army. The only way to save the patient was to cut off the cancerous parts and sterilize the wounds. And it was too late for that, it had metastasized and the knife and radiation and drugs would not be enough. It had all happened so *fast*, a wildfire that started with a match and only moments later was a conflagration. Nobody could have predicted it would erupt so quickly! A year and a half ago, men were supreme on their homeworld, top of the food chain, the king predator. But now . . .

The military minds were not brilliant, they never were, but those in charge were smart enough to know they were losing. All remaining starships were confiscated. Hastily laid plans began to be implemented. There would be a regrouping of key military personnel to the outer colonies, there to develop new plans for combating the aliens.

Sitting in his information center, a cool and clean place of technological miracles of communication, Orona laughed. The Earth was being abandoned. He wouldn't be leaving with them. Oh, he could have gone, but what would be the point? He would survive, but he would have lost the most important battle of his life. There was an ancient custom that sailors had once observed: if a ship sank, the captain went down with it. The aliens had been his project. His work. Someone had spilled a retort of crucial fluid, and the lab had been contaminated. It was his responsibility. He should have foreseen it. Even if everyone else forgot, he never would.

He was going to stay here, win or lose.

The hypersleep chambers stood ready.

"See you in nine months," Wilks said to the others.

The computer locked the ship into its return home. They would be going back faster than they had come, a few months. Wilks hoped things had been kept clean with the alien specimen they had on Earth. They'd be careful, he hoped. And it was only one of them, one couldn't cause too much trouble.

The chambers closed on their patients, lulled them into a rest nearly to the borders of death itself, then held them there in a perfectly balanced stasis.

By the time the first subspace messages of the horrors on Earth finally arrived in the flux of the ship's voyage through the Einsteinian Warp, the remaining few passengers of the *Benedict* were all hard asleep. The ship's computer recorded the cries from Earth, but the computer did not care.

28

Orona stared straight ahead, his face drawn, his expression more tired than anything else. "So, that's the way it is here on Earth," he said. "The military has pulled most of its highest-ranking officers and best remaining troops out, and they are offworld and well into hyperspace by now. A few more installations remain left to evacuate.

"The situation here has deteriorated steadily. Land communications are mostly down, satellite bounce is still working in areas where enough power remains to access it.

"Things are in chaos. In the past months, the aliens have increased their numbers at a rate that seems impossible.

"There are only a few enclaves where security is

holding them off. Perhaps a billion people have died in the last year and a half."

Something pounded on the door behind Orona.

"Even this place, which should have been able to hold out forever, is compromised. Amazing."

The pounding increased.

"I don't know if anybody will see this transmission," he said. "Or that it matters if you do. Such a comedy of errors this whole thing has been. Were I a god, I would be laughing myself silly at man's stupidity."

Thick plastic began to shatter under the force of the hammering.

Orona managed a half smile. He reached into a drawer, came out with a stubby pistol. He looked to his left. Shards of black plastic flew past him, from the unseen fury off the screen. Orona chambered a round in the pistol. Put the muzzle into his mouth. Pulled the trigger.

The back of his head sprayed red and white and he fell forward just as a clawed hand grabbed at him. The talons missed. The alien corrected, then jerked the dead man from the chair like a puppet whose strings have been cut. Shook him.

Another shape moved into view, blocked the camera.

After a moment, Orona was taken away. The room was now empty. The camera ran on, giving a view of the blood and brains and skull spattered onto the wall.

* * *

"Oh, fuck," Billie said, staring at the screen.

Next to her, Wilks nodded, his face grim. "It was all for nothing," he said. "We blew their fucking planet up but it was too late. They were already on Earth. The stupid bastards brought them home and they got loose."

Blake and the crewman stood there, also watching, Bueller lay on a gurney behind Billie.

"What are we going to do, Sarge?"

"Do? What can we do? We're in orbit. We're going down."

Nobody had any better ideas.

Then, the crewman—Parks, his name was—said, "Wilks, we've got company."

"What are you talking about?"

"Check the Doppler screen."

Wilks glanced at it. He swore softly.

It was the elephant-alien's ship, hanging in space only a couple of hundred kilometers away.

Impossible as it was supposed to be in the Einsteinian subspace, the thing had *followed* them.

How?

Why?

"You are cleared for touchdown at these coordinates, *Benedict*. Your computer should do fine, but keep a hand on manual just in case. You veer too much and you land in enemy territory and if you do, you're dinner."

"Thanks a lot, Control," Wilks said into the com. If the computer failed, they were dead; nobody on the ship could pilot a star hopper accurately in atmosphere, certainly not to a pinpoint landing.

"We'd rather you get down in one piece. We need the hardware. Outside of preprogrammed troop carriers, we don't have a lot of birds that can even make orbit."

"Copy, Control. We're on the glide."

Wilks leaned back. Things sounded even worse than the recordings they had seen and heard. Orona's supposedly safe installation had been overrun weeks ago. There didn't seem to be much left to come back for, but Wilks had to see it for himself. His victory on the aliens' homeworld was meaningless now.

When the ship landed, there were dozens of soldiers waiting, guns leveled at them. An officer, a colonel or a general, Billie guessed, strode up and nodded at Wilks.

"We're glad you brought the ship back, Sergeant. We need it. This is the last secure compound remaining. We're bailing out."

"What's going to happen to Earth?"

The man shrugged. "I can't say. I'm supposed to take the rest of my men to the outpost we've established; High Command will sort it out from there."

"You're just going to *leave*? What about the people here?"

The man shook his head. "What I think is, the aliens will overrun everything. Then someday we'll come back and try again. Develop some way to kill 'em from orbit without damaging the land or sea too bad, some kind of biological or chemical thing. We'll start with a clean slate."

Wilks looked as if he were going to punch the man. "There are billions of human beings here!"

"*Were* billions, Sergeant. The aliens have taken a lot of them, a lot have been friendly-fired, a lot died in experiments designed to stop the creatures. There are maybe five, six hundred million left, and going fast. We can't save them. If we're lucky, we'll get clear before this place goes up—"

As if on cue, a junior officer leaned over to the commander. "Sir, pickets report a surge from the southeast. Several thousand bugs attacking. They are through the minefield and approaching the fences."

"Check out the *Benedict*," the officer ordered. "And send C Company to help the pickets."

The armed soldiers swarmed into the ship.

The officer said, "When you think about it, maybe it's not all bad. Earth was on the edge of destruction for a long time. If it hadn't been this, it would have probably been something else that set it off. This way, we can maybe get it right next time."

"What about us?" the crewman asked. Parks, his name was Parks.

"I'm sorry," the officer said, "but there is only so much room. I have my orders."

"Wait," Wilks said. "There's another factor. We had help on the aliens' homeworld. Another space-faring species. He—it saved us."

"So?"

"It followed us here. In its own ship."

"Look, Sergeant, this is all very interesting, but what difference does that make? You think this thing can wipe out all the bugs on the planet?"

"I don't know, but it might help—"

The officer glanced at his chronometer. "If we had the time, yes. But if our intelligence is right, we have got a day, maybe only a few hours before we are overrun. We've set nukes to take out the complex after we've gone. We've lost this war, Sergeant. It's time to retreat."

"Dammit!"

The officer drew his sidearm. "Don't do anything stupid. You can die right now if you do."

Wilks held his hands wide.

Blake, standing between Billie and Bueller on the gurney, moved over a hair. The officer swung his gun to cover her. "I can't let you shoot anybody, General," Blake said.

"Listen, marine, I've been shooting people for months. A few more won't matter."

Blake smiled, and moved toward him.

"Blake, don't!" Wilks said.

But she kept going.

The general fired, his bullet taking Blake square in the chest. Blake hardly paused. The man cursed, fired again—

Wilks jumped. Slammed the heel of his hand into the general's temple just as he swung his pistol around and fired a third round. The bullet *spanged* into the side of the *Benedict*.

Wilks followed the hand strike with his elbow, and a kick as the general fell. He twisted the gun from the man's hand, spun to face the hatch to the ship.

A soldier stepped out. Wilks shot him in the head.

Blake went down. Parks ran off, screaming.

Billie went to the downed android. The downed *woman*.

"Blake . . ."

"Couldn't let him . . . shoot you," she said. She smiled. "Be . . . sure I . . . get my medals, okay, Sarge?"

Wilks glanced at her. "Yeah, kid. No sweat."

Blake's eyes dilated suddenly as Billie watched.

Wilks shook his head. "Damn. Hit her in the main pump. One chance in ten thousand, it's supposed to be caged and almost bulletproof. Must have ricocheted."

Billie said, "Blake!"

"She's gone, Billie," Wilks said. "And we'll be gone too if we don't move our asses, fast! I just killed a general. Go!"

He pulled her up, but she twisted away and grabbed Mitch from his gurney. She slung him onto her back.

"Billie, goddammit!"

"I'll keep up," she said.

Mitch said, "Billie, don't do this—"

"Shut up, Mitch. Otherwise I'll stay here with you and they'll kill me. If you don't want me to do that, then you have to hang on and go with me."

Wilks sprinted away, Billie and her passenger right behind him.

29

When they stopped for breath, Billie said, "Why are we running? There's no place to go. They're going to blow this place up when they leave. Even if there weren't any aliens outside the defenses, we can't get far enough away on foot to escape the blast."

"I don't plan for us to be on foot," he said.

"If what they said is true, nowhere on Earth is any better," Bueller put in.

The three of them were leaning against the inside of a stanchion, a support post that ran from the ground up through the level they were on. Wilks guessed they were on the third level, probably fifty meters above the surface.

"I don't plan for us to be on Earth, either," Wilks said.

"What are you talking about?" That from Billie.

"Remember what the controller said when we left orbit? There are programmed troop carriers here. When they leave, we'll be on one of them."

"How?"

Wilks hefted the general's pistol. "By doing whatever it takes."

Bueller looked uncomfortable. "I'm not supposed to allow that," he said.

Wilks laughed. "How you gonna stop it, gimpy? Besides, I see a basic flaw in your programming here. If they are gonna kill us, me and Billie, and we are gonna kill them, who do you worry about the most?"

Bueller chewed on that for a second. "Billie," he said.

"Ah. So some folks are more important than others, eh?"

"Yes."

"They didn't teach you that in the vats."

"No."

Wilks laughed again. "You just stopped being an android, pal. Welcome to the human race."

Billie allowed Wilks to take Mitch; they could move faster that way, Wilks said. And even as they ran, she marveled over what Mitch had said. He had outgrown his programming. His body might not have been born of a woman, but as far as she was concerned, he was a man.

Wilks led them into a storage area that had a computer terminal. He began punching questions into the system.

"What are you doing?"

He didn't look up at Billie. "Finding out which of the drone ships are carrying crew and which are only lugging cargo. Some will have troops; some will be hauling supplies. We can find a supply ship; we can dump some of 'em and replace the weight with us."

"We don't even know where they are going," Billie said.

"Who cares? Can't be any worse than being fried by atomics or eaten by the monsters."

"Wilks—"

"I know what you are gonna say," he said. "I thought my job was over when I blasted the aliens' homeworld, that I could come back, get stuck away in some nice quiet prison or brainwiped and that would be it. I was looking forward to it. But now, no. I can't quit until every one of these alien bastards is dead."

"Is it worth it?"

"It is to me. A man's got to have a reason to get up in the mornings. I spent years trying to decide if I should just shut my own lights off. Something always kept me from doing it. I never knew what, exactly, but I'm glad it did. I might die, kid, but I am going to go down swinging."

He was as happy as she'd ever seen him. He had a purpose, and that was more than a lot of people had.

"Ah, here we go. A cargo drone, number three-oh-two, nicknamed *The American*. Bay sixteen, level five. Here's the overlay map. . . ."

* * *

They approached the docked ships cautiously. Wilks put Bueller down carefully and drew the handgun. "I'll just wound the guards," he said, "I won't kill them."

"Thank you," Bueller said.

"Stay here. I'll be back when I'm done." He started to leave. Paused. "Hey, Bueller, I never got around to telling you how good a job you and your troops did. You did okay."

"For an android?" Bueller said.

"Nah, for anybody."

Wilks eased his way onto the dock, using the supports as cover. In the end, it was easy. There were four guards, they had their weapons slung, they weren't expecting trouble. When he was close enough and still covered, Wilks took a deep breath, brought the pistol up, and quickly fired four times. The suppressed barrel cut most of the noise.

He hit each of the four guards once.

Right between the eyes.

Head shots were the best way for an instant knockdown.

So he lied to Bueller. Life was hard.

Billie saw Wilks coming back. "Our ride is here, people. Let's go."

He led them past the bodies of four soldiers who had been guarding the ship.

Mitch looked at the dead men.

"Sorry. My hand must have slipped," Wilks said.

Mitch shrugged. Once they were dead, his responsibility ended. Wilks had to know that.

Behind them, small-arms fire rattled. It didn't sound close, but it wasn't too far away, either.

"Looks like company has come calling," Wilks said. "I'd bet the schedule is going to be advanced just a tad."

The ship was a rectangular module with heat tiles on the bottom and a small control cab that looked vaguely like the head of a giant insect stuck on the front. It seemed almost an afterthought to Billie, the way the cab joined the brick-shaped body of the ship.

Wilks caught her look. "Cobbled together out of spare parts," he said. "We'll be lucky if it doesn't come apart when we lift. Come on. We've got to move some gear around. This bird is loaded with food supplies and frozen sperm and ova, regular little Noah's ark. We have to install an oxy plant and recycling and recovery system so we can breathe and have a way to clear wastes. And since I don't know how long we'll be in flight, some sleep chambers would be nice, too. Take us a couple of hours, I've located the stuff we need on the ship next door."

"What about the passengers on that ship?" Mitch asked.

"They can double up in the chambers if they have to. This bird doesn't have any 'cause it's meant to be crewless. We need 'em more than they do."

It took almost two and a half hours to get the proper gear installed, and would have been impossible without the dumbots Wilks rounded up.

The sounds of combat were drawing much closer

as they finished. He could hear the occasional rico-
chet *ching* off the alien armor, and whoever had
taken over from the dead general would probably
be hauling ass real soon now.

Every now and then, Wilks heard a man or
woman scream.

Yeah. Real soon now.

"Let's lock it up," he said to Billie. "I have a
feeling we'll be going for a ride any minute."

The control cabin still had acceleration couches
in place, they hadn't gotten around to stripping
them, so Wilks helped Billie cinch Bueller into place
before he went to his own couch. He didn't know
exactly where the retreat was going, but he had
rigged the sleep chambers so they could climb in
when they hit hyperspace; the automatics would
shut the things down when they dropped back into
normal space. After that, well, they'd see.

No sooner had he fastened his own restraints
than the ship's board lit up with launch readings.
Close.

"Hang on," he said. "Looks like somebody just lit
the fuses."

30

The ship lifted, and the high-gee force shoved at the passengers, pressing them deep into the cushioned seats. Wilks supposed that if he had a viewer operational, he would have looked back, although it would surely be a depressing sight. Watching your own planet being overrun by monsters wasn't what he would call fun.

There was nothing to be done for it, now, at least.

The first rule in winning a war was to survive. If you lived, you could fight another day. Dead, you couldn't do shit.

And Wilks planned to stay alive as long as it took to kill those things. As long as it took.

Whoever had programmed the ships had figured on using Earth's gravity to help sling them into deep space. The cargo drone reached high orbit and the drives pulsed, pushing them into an ellipse. The monitors showed that there were at least fifty ships in the loose formation. Plus one unidentified vessel whose configurations Wilks recognized.

"Hey, say good-bye to old longnose," he said.

Billie looked at him. Went blank. Then screamed.

Somehow Mitch managed to unhook himself from his seat and walk on his hands to where Billie was still strapped into her chair. He climbed up, held her, tried to reach her.

"Billie! What is it? Billie?"

It was inside her brain again, that alien presence she'd last felt light-years away. The thing that had saved them from the monsters.

It was laughing.

The force of its thoughts overwhelmed her, she couldn't stop them, it was like trying to halt an ocean breaker with a bucket. The feelings were mixed: it gloated, it was filled with snide joy, it lusted, it felt superior, it hated, it raged, and among all those were things she couldn't identify, feelings for which there was no human reference.

But she got enough of it to know what it wanted her to know.

Oh, God!

"Billie?"

She managed to focus on Mitch. Mitch, who loved her. Her feelings for him became like a wall, against which the alien spacefarer's emotional sea splashed. Some of it slipped past, but enough was stopped so Billie could recover her senses. Somehow it knew this. The tide stopped.

"It—that thing. It talked to me."

"What did it say?" Wilks put in.

"It has no more use for us than it did the aliens. It followed us here to see our world, to see if there was anything here worth taking. It wants to conquer us."

"Won't have a lot of opposition, will it?" Wilks said.

"It plans to wait and let the aliens kill all the humans. Then when the soldiers come back—it knows their plans—it will be waiting. Maybe with others of its own kind. To take Earth from the winners."

"Damn," Wilks said. "If it isn't one thing, it's another. Out of the hurricane and into a tornado."

After that, there wasn't much any of them could say.

Wilks had the sleep chambers cycling on line; according to his instruments, the ship was about to enter subspace. None of them knew for how long or how far they would travel while dancing in the nowhere and nowhen of the Einsteinian Warp. It didn't really matter.

Billie helped Wilks install Mitch into his chamber. Wilks moved away to check his own bed for the long sleep. Billie stood over Mitch, smiled down at him.

"You okay?" he asked.

"Yes. I am."

They embraced, a long, soulful hug, then she stepped away and triggered the system. The lid clamshelled down and sealed. Mitch kept his eyes open, watching her, until the gases put him under.

She watched him sleep for a moment, then turned toward her own chamber.

Wilks was already climbing into his. He waved at her.

Well. She had come a long way in her life. From one destroyed planet to another, to yet another. But she was still alive. Not so long ago, that wouldn't have meant much to Billie, but things had changed. She had Mitch now, somehow they would find a way to repair him, bring him back to what he'd been before.

No, that wasn't true. He was already more than he'd been before, even if his body was half-destroyed. But there were ways to fix that, easier because of what he was. And even that wasn't really important.

Billie climbed into her chamber. Touched a control. Watched the lid fan slowly down. No, what was important was, she wasn't alone anymore.

And she knew as sleep claimed her, she would not dream of the past and of monsters. Rather she would dream of the future. Whatever that might be. After all, they hadn't done too bad so far. A war was fought one battle at a time.

Billie smiled, and closed her eyes.

STEVE PERRY has written dozens of science fiction and fantasy novels, the most recent of which is SPINDOC, along with several of the bestselling *Aliens*™ novelizations, alone and in collaboration with his daughter, Stephani. He has also written a number of animated teleplays, including among them several for the *Batman* series, as well as numerous short stories and articles. He lives in Beaverton, Oregon, with his wife, who publishes a small monthly newspaper.